...petition by describing he...
an exotic island by a gorgeous and powerful man.
Little did she realise that she'd just wandered into
her dream job! Today she writes for Mills & Boon,
featuring often stubborn but always *to die for* heroes
and the women who bring them to their knees. She
believes that the best books are those you never want
to end. Just like life…

Also by Sharon Kendrick

The Billionaire's Defiant Acquisition
Crowned for the Prince's Heir
Di Sione's Virgin Mistress
A Royal Vow of Convenience
Secrets of a Billionaire's Mistress
The Sheikh's Bought Wife
The Pregnant Kavakos Bride
The Italian's Christmas Secret

The Bond of Billionaires miniseries

Claimed for Makarov's Baby
The Sheikh's Christmas Conquest

Discover more at millsandboon.co.uk

BOUND TO THE SICILIAN'S BED

SHARON KENDRICK

MILLS & BOON

First Published in Great Britain 2018
by Mills & Boon, an imprint of HarperCollins*Publishers*
1 London Bridge Street, London, SE1 9GF

© 2018 Sharon Kendrick

ISBN: 978-0-263-93414-4

MIX
Paper from
responsible sources
FSC® C007454

This book is produced from independently certified FSC™ paper
to ensure responsible forest management.
For more information visit www.harpercollins.co.uk/green.

Printed and bound in Spain
by CPI, Barcelona

For darling Pete Crone, who is a constant inspiration to this sometimes (!) frazzled writer, and has many of the attributes of the romantic hero.

And for Charlie Bell, director at Vardags— the amazing law firm with the amazing view over London—who provided invaluable help for this story.

CHAPTER ONE

ROCCO BARBERI FELT anger pumping through his veins and it was enough to stop him in his tracks. Because he didn't *do* anger. He was known as a man of cool calculation. His implacable Sicilian features were notorious for never betraying a flicker of emotion and his business rivals often said he would have made a world-class poker player. So why was rage flooding through him like hot lava as he stood outside a tiny art shop in some God-forsaken Cornish town?

He knew why. Because of her. His wife. His mouth twisted. His *estranged* wife. The woman who was standing inside the shop studying some sort of vase, her thick dark curls cascading down her back, leading the eye naturally to her narrow waist and the luscious curve of her bottom. The woman who had walked away from him without a qualm, uncaring of his reputation and everything he had done for her.

He pushed open the door and the doorbell jangled loudly as he walked in. He saw her look up, her face freezing with shock—and Rocco enjoyed a brief moment of pleasure as he read disbelief in those green eyes,

which had once so bewitched him. He heard her suck
in an unsteady breath and as she put the vase down he
noticed her fingers were trembling. Good, he thought
grimly. *Good.*

'Rocco,' she said breathlessly and he could see her
throat constricting as she swallowed. That long, pale
neck he had once covered in urgent kisses before moving on to the infinitely softer territory of her breasts.
'What…what are you doing here?'

The deliberate pause he allowed was just long enough
to increase the sudden tension, which had gathered like
a storm cloud in the small shop. 'You've just served me
with divorce papers, Nicole,' he drawled. 'What did you
think would happen? That I would just sign over half
my fortune and let you walk off into the sunset with a
toss of your pretty curls? Is that what you were hoping?'

She was brushing a dark spiral of hair away from a
face flushed pink—acting with the self-consciousness
of a woman who was uncertain about her appearance
and Rocco was unprepared for the sudden wave of lust
which washed over him. Would she have taken a little
more care with her clothes if she'd known he was coming—worn something a little more flattering than those
faded jeans and a filmy white shirt, which concealed
far too much of those luscious breasts?

'Of course I wasn't,' she answered, still in that faintly
breathless voice. 'I just thought…'

'Yes?' His voice rang out flatly and he saw her flinch.

'That you might have given me some kind of warning.'

'You mean, like you did when you walked away from
our marriage?'

'Rocco—'

'Or when your lawyer sent me those papers last week?' he continued relentlessly. 'You didn't even do me the courtesy of a phone call to let me know you were about to file for divorce, did you, Nicole? Which naturally led me to the conclusion that you were the kind of woman who favoured surprises. So here I am,' he finished softly. 'Your big surprise.'

Nicole felt dizzy. Faint. And not just because of the steely accusations which were slicing through the air towards her. She met the blaze of his eyes and wondered how, after just a few seconds in his company, she was already feeling mixed up and at a disadvantage. She hadn't seen Rocco Barberi for two whole years yet his impact was as devastating as it had ever been. Maybe even more so. She'd forgotten the way he could dominate the space around him and make any room seem to shrink whenever he walked in. She'd forgotten because she'd forced herself to forget the man she had loved even though duty had been the only thing on *his* mind when he'd slipped that wedding band on her finger. She licked her lips. Maybe she'd been foolish to expect anything deeper when their relationship had been doomed from the start—because those kinds of relationships always were. Rich man/poor girl was all very well in theory, but in practice...

She thought about the fuss which had surrounded their unlikely marriage and all the lurid newspaper headlines which had been splashed around. It had been a big story at the time. *'Sicilian Billionaire Weds Cleaner'*—and the inevitable: *'Fairy Tale Marriage*

Turns Sour'. And then it had ended as abruptly as it had begun. She'd walked away from him and their marriage because she'd needed to. The gulf between them had widened to such a distance that she'd known there was no going back, and when she'd lost the baby there had been no reason for them to be together any more. She'd needed to break free in order to survive.

She had told herself that over and over again in those early days after she'd left Sicily. At first every painful minute had seemed like an eternity but gradually the days had drifted into weeks and eventually months. She hadn't taken Rocco's phone calls or answered his letters because she'd known that a clean break was the only way she would have the courage to end it, although it had felt like torture at the time. When the months had turned into years she'd assumed Rocco had accepted they were better off apart, just as she had done. Yet here he was, just turning up out of the blue. In her shop and in her life. It felt as if someone were crushing her heart between their fingers. It brought the pain of the past rushing back so fast that she had to remember to breathe.

And that was what she needed to focus on—her brief tenure as Rocco's wife. The reality—not the fairy tale, which had never really existed anyway. When even her choice of clothes had been dictated by the influential Sicilian billionaire who had treated her like an old-fashioned chattel he'd been forced to purchase against his better judgement.

But that didn't stop her looking at him. From letting her gaze drift over his muscular physique, clad today in one of those expensive charcoal suits he favoured, which emphasised every honed sinew of his remarkable body. Her throat dried as she registered the pale shirt which contrasted so vividly with his olive skin. Had she hoped she might have acquired some kind of immunity to him in the intervening years? Of course she had—because hope was the one emotion which defied logic, the one which could make you get up in the morning and put one foot in front of the other no matter how dark the world seemed outside. Yet Rocco seemed even more dazzling than she remembered— as if absence had only added an extra dimension to his powerful sexuality.

His glowing skin was dark and his startling blue eyes spoke of a distant Greek ancestry. Eyes which could fell you with a single look. Which could undress you in seconds before his hands accomplished the task far more efficiently. The last time she'd seen him Nicole had felt numb with pain and an emptiness which had left little room for anything else.

But now?

She could feel the erratic thumping of her heart. There was no such numbness now. Her senses felt as if he'd kick-started them into life without even trying. She could feel it in the prickle of her breasts and the molten rush of heat to her belly. A familiar restlessness entered her body as it shivered into life and memories of being in his arms were enough to bring a renewed flush of colour to her cheeks. But those thoughts and feelings were nothing but a distraction—as well as a waste of time. There was no point in desiring Rocco. She was nothing to him and she never had been. Just the woman he'd married who had failed to give him the child she'd been carrying. It was over. It had never really begun. So don't prolong it or drag it out and make it any worse than it needs to be. Keep it cool and businesslike.

'So what can I do for you, Rocco?' She looked at him enquiringly, trying to keep her expression neutral. 'Is there something in particular you wanted to discuss with me—and if so, don't you think it might be better done through our lawyers?'

'I'm here,' he said slowly, 'because I think we might be able to do each other a favour.'

She studied him warily. 'I don't understand. We're separated—and separating people don't really do each other favours.'

Rocco ran the edge of his thumb over his bottom lip. He was fully aware that some people might describe what he was about to do as emotional blackmail—but so what? Didn't his shallow, green-eyed wife deserve everything she was going to get? He felt the beat of a pulse at his temple. Wasn't it time she discovered that you didn't cross Rocco Barberi unless you were prepared to pay the price? That was why he had come here today, intending to tell her exactly what he wanted, knowing she would be forced to grant him his wish if she wanted her damned divorce.

He'd thought it would be easy. Straightforward. A simple equation of A + B = C. But he had failed to factor in desire, hadn't he? A desire which had taken him completely by surprise. He had imagined he would look at her as he might any other ex-lover—with a cool impartiality, which had always served him well in the past, because once you had repeatedly tasted a woman's body your appetite for her inevitably diminished. But that wasn't happening. He wondered what it was about her which was making him grow as hard as rock, so he was having difficulty concentrating on anything other than what it would feel like to be deep inside her again— riding her until she shuddered out his name. Was it because she had once worn his wedding band and the significance of that went deeper than he'd imagined?

His voice became hard. 'I need you to do something for me.'

'Sorry, Rocco. You're talking to the wrong person.' She shook her head so that all those thick dark curls shimmered around her shoulders. 'I don't have to do anything for you. We're getting divorced. Remember?'

'Maybe we are,' he answered softly. 'Or maybe not.'

She blinked at him in consternation. 'But the law says we can divorce after two years of living apart.'

'I know what the law says. But that can happen only with the agreement of both parties.' There was a pause. 'Think about it, Nicole. You need my consent to terminate our marriage. I could drag it out for years if I wanted.'

As she heard the unmistakable threat behind his words, Nicole's instinct was to turn and run. To run so far that he'd never be able to find her. Until she reminded herself that instinct had never served her well where Rocco was concerned. It had led her into his arms and into his bed, even though she'd known deep inside that he'd only wanted her for sex. And she had been right, hadn't she?

But she was no longer that woman. The star-struck virgin who had allowed her powerful boss to seduce her. Who had fallen victim to the practised heaven of his touch. The innocent young cleaner who had believed the smooth lies which had flowed from his sensual lips and allowed herself to be guided by them. Who had obediently worn the crotchless panties he'd bought for her from shops in London's Soho and bucked with pleasure when he'd slid his fingers inside them. She'd even pretended to enjoy the light lash of a whip caressing her bare buttocks because she had wanted to bring him as much pleasure as he brought her. Because she had wanted to *please* him. To be his perfect lover in the hope that one day he might care for her as much as she'd begun to care for him. Yet soon after she'd given him her virginity, Rocco had begun to distance himself. Had started avoiding her at work. Suddenly there had been pressing business trips which had desperately needed his attention—something which apparently was a ploy of his when he was trying to get some needy lover off his back.

In fact, he probably would have gone out of his way never to have seen her again if nature hadn't intervened and cast them both in the unexpected roles of parents-to-be. She swallowed as the painful memories crowded into her mind and tried to remind herself that was all in the past. Things were different now. She was getting used to life as a single woman. And yes, it was a struggle to exist on the pittance she earned from this little art shop she'd opened with the help of a grant from the local council—but at least she was following her dreams instead of living a nightmare. She didn't need Rocco Barberi or his billions—or his cold, emotionless heart.

Drawing her shoulders back, she tilted her chin to meet his sapphire gaze. 'Why on earth wouldn't you give me your consent when we both know our marriage is over?'

'Is that why you didn't answer any of my letters? Because you'd come to that decision all on your own?'

'It was what we both knew in our hearts!' she defended. 'I just couldn't see the point in dragging it out any longer.'

His body tensed and he opened his mouth to respond when the sound of the shop bell punctured the atmosphere as a middle-aged woman opened the door. Did she pick up on the fraught atmosphere? Was that why she glanced uncertainly from Rocco to Nicole as if she were gate-crashing a private party?

'I'm sorry,' she said, automatically prefacing her sentence with the ever-present apology of the English. 'Are you—?'

'We're closed,' said Rocco shortly, watching as Nicole opened her mouth to protest—but by then it was too late because the woman had scuttled out again, murmuring yet more words of apology.

And then his estranged wife turned on him, all her studied politeness a distant memory, her emerald eyes spitting fire at him.

'You can't do that!' she declared indignantly. 'You

can't just march into *my* shop and order prospective customers to leave!'

'I just did,' he said, without any hint of apology. 'So let me put this to you carefully, just so that there can be no misunderstanding. You have a choice, Nicole. Either I turn the shop sign around to say you're closed, or you agree to meet me when you've finished work. Because I don't want any more interruptions like that when I put my proposition to you.'

'Proposition?'

'That's what I said.'

'And if I refuse?'

'Why would you refuse? You want your freedom, don't you? The precious freedom which is so important to you. It might be in your best interests to…what is it that you English say?' He rubbed a reflective finger over the hint of stubble at his chin. 'Ah, yes. *To keep me sweet.*'

Nicole felt herself stiffen because his voice had taken on that velvety caress which used to have her hurling herself into his arms and raining kiss after kiss all over his rugged features. Well, not any more. That ship had sailed. No matter how much her body might be longing to feel him close to her again, she was going to fight that attraction with every fibre of her being. And he was right. Another customer might walk in and it didn't look very professional to have a divorcing couple slugging out their differences. Surely it wouldn't hurt her to listen to what he had to say. To humour him a little in order to facilitate her freedom.

'Okay,' she said, with a sigh. 'How about I meet you

for a coffee when I've finished work? There's a café at the far end of the harbour which will still be open. It's got a red and white awning at the front—you can't miss it. I'll see you in there.'

'No.' He shook his head and his mouth hardened. 'I'm not meeting you in public in some damned *café*. I want to visit your apartment, Nicole. To see for myself the place you have chosen above your Sicilian home.'

It was on the tip of Nicole's tongue to tell him that the lavish Barberi complex had felt more like a prison than a home, but what was the point of upping the ante? Mightn't it drive home how serious she was about this divorce if she showed Rocco where she lived? Mightn't he get it into his stubborn head that wealth and privilege meant nothing, not when you measured those things against peace of mind?

'Very well, I live in the flat above the tea shop on Greystone Road. Number thirty-seven,' she said grudgingly. 'But don't come before seven.'

'*Capisce.*' He nodded his dark head.

He was just on his way to the door when he paused in front of a small display of pottery, picking up one of the pieces to study it. It was a glowing terracotta jug with a handle fashioned to look like the twisted leaves on a lemon branch. Raised yellow fruits dotted the surface and in the background was the flash of blue—an artistic representation of the distant sea. Slowly he turned it around in his olive fingers to study it, before glancing up to meet her eyes.

'This is good,' he said slowly. 'It reminds me of Sicily.'

She nodded, the sudden clench of her heart making

her wish he hadn't made the connection. 'That's what inspired me.'

'Perhaps I should buy it,' he reflected. 'You certainly look as if you could do with a few more customers.'

'Particularly when you drive away the ones I do have,' she observed acidly. 'Anyway, it's not for sale.'

She pointed to a bright red sticker, though in reality nobody had bought it, because it had never actually been for sale. It was the last remaining piece of the collection she'd made when she'd returned from Sicily, feeling heartbroken and empty. Her bestselling collection, as it happened, but she wouldn't tell him that. Just as she wouldn't tell him about the tiny, hand-embroidered romper suit she'd bought soon after she'd had her first pregnancy scan, which was lying shrouded in tissue paper in one of her bedroom drawers. She was planning to sell the jug just as soon as the ink was dry on her divorce papers. The romper suit she suspected she would never be able to part with.

He replaced the piece and all Nicole was aware of were those amazing sapphire eyes searing into her. He was always the most beautiful man she had ever seen and nothing about that had changed. He could still make her heart beat fast. Still make her shiver and her breasts swell into vibrant life against her lacy bra. Just as he reminded her of the darkest time in her life and her fear that she would never be able to recover. But she *had* recovered. And she'd done it without him—because they were no good for each other. She had accepted that. It was time that Rocco did, too.

And suddenly she wanted him out of the shop, before

she gave into the pain which was welling up inside her and threatening to spill over. Before it dissolved into bitter tears, which would remind her of everything she had lost.

CHAPTER TWO

Two cups of herbal tea and a stern reminder that getting emotional would accomplish nothing meant Nicole's nerves were less jangled by the time she arrived home to find Rocco waiting outside her apartment. She'd told herself that getting sucked in by dark memories wasn't going to help anyone. She'd told herself she needed to be calm and impartial when it came to dealing with Rocco, but maybe that was just too big an ask with a man like him.

She thought how out of place he looked in the narrow Cornish street, his powerful body drawing attention away from the cute little houses which surrounded him. Every property had window boxes full of colourful flowers dancing in the breeze, but her estranged husband was a study in unmoving darkness—the whiteness of his silk shirt the only thing lightening his shadowed body and rugged features. Her heart began to pound as she walked towards him.

The usual batch of holidaymakers was spilling out from the tea room below her tiny apartment and others were strolling along the pavement on their way to eat fish and chips, or drink dark pints of bitter in one of the iconic little pubs close by. Yet every person turned to glance at Rocco—men and women alike—as if recognising the powerful stranger in their midst. And even though he was head of one of the world's biggest pharmaceutical companies and one of the world's wealthiest men, Nicole suspected he would have attracted attention even if he possessed nothing. And she mustn't forget that. She mustn't forget that underneath all her swarm of painful feelings, she was as susceptible to him as the next woman.

And he could hurt her all over again.

His sapphire eyes were fixed on her and Nicole felt stupidly self-conscious as she reached him.

'You're early,' she said, reaching into her bag for her keys.

'You know what it's like. I couldn't keep away,' he said mockingly.

She gave a tight smile. 'Then you'd better come in.'

Rocco stood back to let her pass, unable to stop himself from reacting to her unique scent as she pushed open the front door, a scent which had nothing to do with perfume. It was the essence of *her*, which he had once found so intoxicating. Still did, if he was being honest—and he really hadn't expected that. But then, Nicole had a talent for making him do the unexpected, didn't she? Her green-eyed look of provocation had lured him into breaking every rule in the book, just as her abundance of curves had made her seem more feminine than any woman he'd ever met.

When he'd seduced her he'd thought she was experienced. Why wouldn't he—when she'd flirted like crazy with him after their initial meeting? Yet he hadn't touched her until their fourth date, something which was unheard of for him. Despite the fact that she'd clearly wanted him—what woman didn't?—he'd forced himself to wait. He still wasn't sure why. Maybe he'd just wanted to delay gratification for as long as possible, in an attempt to preserve that delicious state of desire she had aroused in him.

And then he'd discovered she had been a virgin and that had been a whole new ballgame. It had blown him away. Intimacy with Nicole Watson had eclipsed every other sexual encounter he'd ever had and Rocco was tempted to pull her into his arms to see whether she felt as good as he remembered. To lose himself in her soft and feminine body and thrust into the wet heat which had always awaited him.

But she had deserted him.

She had thrown everything back in his face.

The memory of that was enough to dissolve his desire as he followed her up a rickety old staircase—unable to prevent the moue of scorn which escaped his lips as he entered the cramped living room. His mouth twisted. She had chosen to live *here*? A Barberi occupying a place such as this? Why, a medieval servant would have boasted of something finer!

He looked around. It was small. Unbelievably small. A tiny sofa had been covered with a brightly coloured throw—but nothing could disguise the battered surface beneath. There was a sagging armchair, an old-fashioned electric fire and an archway leading into a cubbyhole of a kitchen. And that was it.

The only photograph on show was an old one he recognised of her mother but there were none of him. Rocco's mouth hardened. Did he really think there might have been? Perhaps a shot of them standing outside the Sicilian cathedral, a white tulle veil billowing around her dark curls and Nicole's flat stomach concealing the fact that she was several weeks pregnant?

His jaw tightened as he wondered what had made him start thinking about such a taboo subject but, with the ruthlessness born of practice, he pushed the powerful image to the back of his mind as he stared at the woman in front of him, thinking how different she looked. Gone were the elegant clothes which had crammed her wardrobe during their short marriage and in their place was the distinctly Bohemian look she had always favoured. Clothes he had found attractive enough in a mistress, but which had been unsuitable for a Barberi wife. Silver hoops gleamed amid the wild tumble of dark curls and the lush sensuality of her mouth was fixed and unsmiling as she returned his stare.

'So,' she said. 'What exactly is this all about, Rocco?'

He thought of chastising her for her lack of courtesy. He had lifted her out of the gutter and given her the chance of a better life. He had taught her everything. *Everything.* What to wear and how to behave. When to speak and when to remain silent. And now she was treating him with the barely disguised impatience she might show a persistent salesman who had shoved his foot in the door.

'You don't even offer me coffee?' he drawled.

'There won't be time. I wasn't planning a long visit. Were you?' She looked at him enquiringly. 'You told me you had something you wanted to say, so why don't you just say it?'

He sat down on the arm of the sofa, stretching his long legs out in front of him. 'I need you to play a part for me,' he said.

'A part?' she echoed non-comprehendingly. 'What are you talking about?'

'As my wife.' He gave a mirthless smile. 'Or rather, my reconciling wife.'

'Your reconciling *wife*? Are you crazy?'

Rocco thought back to the number of times he had asked himself the same question, wondering how he could have fallen for someone like her. Why, despite the eager attentions of women of his own class, he had allowed himself to become transfixed by this one—a humble cleaner at his London headquarters. Because of her he had behaved in a way which still had the power to make him shudder as he remembered locking the door to his office and taking her over his desk. He remembered her curving hips facing upwards in a silent plea for him to remove her panties. And him complying with shaking hands, his fingers sliding over her molten heat, before entering her with a hunger so all-consuming that it had completely blown his mind. He swallowed. All his legendary self-control had deserted him the moment he'd laid a finger on her. The powerful head of Barberi associates thrusting hungrily into one of his lowly employees, with his trousers around his ankles like a teenager!

He swallowed before shaking his head. 'On the contrary, *tesoro*—I'm deadly serious. This petition could not have come at a worse time for me.'

'Really?'

'Yes, really. I'm in the middle of a deal, which is balancing on a knife-edge right now.'

'Gosh. I thought you had a hundred per cent success rate where business was concerned. You must be slipping, Rocco.'

He gave an impatient flicker of a smile. 'This deal is a big one,' he said softly. 'The biggest in a long time. I'm attempting a hostile takeover bid of a European company, which will increase my stock to make Barberi the biggest pharmaceutical business in the world.'

'So what's the problem?'

His eyes narrowed as he met her gaze. 'The problem is that there has been some opposition to my involvement. Several of the shareholders have hired a PR agency to see what dirt they can dig up on me and a complicated personal life could provide fuel for their stories. Plus, one of the biggest shareholders is a man named Marcel Dupois who's known for being extremely conservative, particularly around family matters.' He shifted his weight slightly. 'The last thing I need is an estranged wife coming out of the woodwork seeking a divorce at such a sensitive time.'

'So drop your business bid.'

'But I don't want to drop it.' His voice hardened. 'It's too important to me.'

Nicole nodded. Of course it was. Business had always been important to Rocco. The only thing which really mattered in his life. His go-to activity which took precedence over everything else, even his wife. Especially his wife. 'So what are you expecting me to do—call off the divorce?'

'Only temporarily.'

'I wasn't being serious, Rocco.'

'But I am.' His sapphire eyes flattened. 'Deadly serious.'

'You want me to delay the petition.'

'I want you to play a role. You were always very good at role-play, weren't you, Nicole? It's easy. All you have to do is pretend to be my wife for a couple of days.'

'Pretend to be your wife,' she repeated slowly.

'Sure. I have a high-profile weekend coming up and having you by my side as my loving spouse could be extremely useful.'

'Useful?'

'You don't like the word?'

Nicole bristled. Of course she didn't like the word, which seemed to emphasise the only thing she'd ever been to him. Someone who was convenient. Who could be picked up and put down like a commodity. She wanted to push him towards the door. To tell him to get out and never come back—until she remembered what her lawyer had said just before he'd filed the papers.

'Your husband is a powerful man, Mrs Barberi. Not a man you'd want to get into a protracted legal battle with. Not under any circumstances. My advice to you is to keep proceedings as amicable as possible.'

She got that, but even so.

Masquerade as his *wife*?

Open herself up to all that pain and frustration and make even more of a mockery of their doomed marriage?

No way.

She shook her head.

'It's a crazy suggestion. You must realise that. I'm sorry you've come all this way for nothing, Rocco, but I can't do it.'

He looked around the small scruffy room before returning his gaze to her. 'I meant what I said, Nicole,' he said. 'Unless you were prepared to cooperate, I might not let you have your divorce.'

She shook her head. 'You can't stop me.'

'Oh, but I can,' he argued softly. 'We've been separated for two years but you still need my agreement.' There was a pause. 'I've spoken to my lawyers and I can easily defend the petition by saying I don't believe the marriage has broken down irretrievably.'

'You wouldn't…' she breathed.

'Wouldn't I? I would do whatever it takes to make this deal, Nicole.' His eyes gleamed. 'The choice is yours, *tesoro*.'

Nicole heard the steely determination behind his words and thought about his power and influence. Her lawyer had been right—Rocco could do exactly what he wanted because he had limitless funds to support him, and she didn't. Simple as that. In theory she *could* wait for her divorce—but she didn't want to. Three more years of being tied to Rocco Barberi with all the memories that brought with it? Of feeling that something was always holding her back from living her life? Of being unable to stop those rugged features and sapphire eyes from invading her dreams every night? No way.

Slowly, she lifted her eyes to his. 'And if I agreed? What would it entail?'

He didn't react. There was no triumph on his face. His expression was as coolly impassive as ever it had been. Of course it was, Nicole told herself bitterly. Rocco didn't change. He was still the same cold-hearted control freak he'd ever been.

'You will accompany me to a film screening, a dinner and a cocktail party over the course of a couple of days, that's all.'

'That's all,' she repeated slowly.

'*Se*. We pretend we're giving our marriage another go. We become yet another couple who've come unstuck and are trying to solve our "issues". Everyone likes a love story and it will show a more *sympathetic* side to my character.' His eyes gleamed mockingly. 'You get a weekend in Monaco and I get my deal.'

'Monaco?'

'That's where I live now.'

She stared at him in surprise. 'Not Sicily?'

'Not any more.'

She wondered whether she had imagined the sudden bleakness in his voice, but Nicole's head was too full to wonder why he had left his beloved homeland. She tried sifting through her options as he stared at her and wondered if she could go through with his crazy plan.

Yet how ironic was it that she needed to put on a convincing performance as his reconciling wife, in order to gain her freedom from that very role?

Could she pull it off?

In public, maybe—but in private... Her tongue slid over the sudden parchment-dry surface of her lower lip. Because yes, they might still be at war but things were never that simple. They never were with Rocco. He'd been the only man she'd ever really wanted and she was fast discovering that he still was.

And even though he hadn't given a single indication that he might feel the same way about her, there was no knowing what was going on in that unfathomable mind of his. If Rocco still felt a flicker of the desire she was feeling right now—what then? If he should turn all that blazing Sicilian charm on her, would she be capable of resisting it?

Resisting *him*?

She had no choice. She didn't want her heart broken all over again and therefore she mustn't allow her sexy husband anywhere near her. All she needed to do was remember just how bad the pain had been and how much it had hurt to walk away.

She shook her head. 'I can't do it, Rocco,' she said, swallowing down the emotion which was threatening to make her voice tremble. 'You must be able to see that.'

But if she was hoping for understanding or for a modicum of consideration then she was about to be disappointed, because his features darkened into a look of determination she recognised only too well. He nodded and glanced at his watch as if he was late for a meeting, before giving a careless shrug of his shoulders.

'Then it looks like I'll see you in court, Nicole,' he said softly.

And she believed him. Rocco wasn't a man who said things he didn't mean. He was a man who had the power to do exactly what he wanted and if that involved using a wife he had never loved to further his business ambitions, then he would do it. He had her in a corner. He knew it and she knew it, too. Nicole's heart was racing as she met his brilliant gaze, unable to keep the anger from her voice. 'Very well,' she said. 'Since you leave me no choice... I'll do it.'

Rocco nodded, his senses on alert as he registered her reluctant agreement. He had achieved what he had set out to achieve but now he found himself wondering why she was prepared to do something she clearly detested, just to get her damned divorce.

'So why the rush to the lawyers?' he questioned silkily. He cast a disdainful eye around the room. 'Can't wait to get your hands on my money? Did you wake up one morning and decide that this shabby little place simply wasn't for you? Did you think your wealthy husband ought to provide you with a settlement which would enable you to get out of here—is that what this is all about, Nicole?'

She shook her head. 'It's not about the money, Rocco. I'm not planning to bleed you dry, if that's what you're hinting at.'

'No?' And then something else suddenly occurred to him—and Rocco was startled by the powerful streak of jealousy which flooded through him like dark poison. Because he had thought he was over her. He had decided that from the moment he had arrived back from the States and discovered she'd left him. 'Then maybe it's something else, something rather more common in these situations.'

'What are you talking about?'

'Perhaps there's a new man on the horizon and you want to be free for him. Is that what it is, my little temptress?' His voice hardened as he allowed the thought to grow and suddenly he could see yet another benefit to making her work for her divorce. Because if Nicole *did* have a new lover, then wouldn't that lover be outraged to learn she was spending the weekend with Rocco Barberi? He felt a sudden punch of sadistic pleasure. 'Perhaps you've already started a relationship and he's telling you to get rid of your Sicilian husband pretty damned quick.'

If Nicole had been feeling more genial she might have laughed in his face. For a start, no other man had even looked at her since she'd left her husband, mainly, she suspected, because she was giving out such negative vibes. But even if they had—even in the unlikely event of some gorgeous man sashaying into her little art shop and asking her on a date—it would have left her completely cold. Because no other man could ever be Rocco and he was the only man she'd ever wanted and sometimes she worried that was never going to change. Was that going to be another lasting legacy from her failed marriage—an inability to forget him?

But he doesn't need to know that, she told herself

fiercely. He doesn't need to know anything about you. Defiantly, she met his questioning gaze.

'My reasons are mine and mine alone,' she said coolly. 'And they are none of your business, Rocco.'

CHAPTER THREE

SO THIS WAS MONACO.

Stepping from the private jet, Nicole felt the warmth of the sun beating down on her head as she looked around, narrowing her eyes behind her sunglasses. In the distance she could see the bright blue blaze of the Mediterranean with fancy white and silver yachts bobbing on the glittering sapphire water.

She'd never been here before but she knew all about the sun-drenched principality at the tip of southern France, which was home to some of the richest people in the world. A place of luxury and excess and glamour. Her heart gave a funny twist. And now it was Rocco's home, too. She pushed her sunglasses further up her nose. Strange to think of him living in this billionaires' playground when he'd always been so fiercely loyal to his homeland and its rustic values. When he'd insisted that simple pleasures were what turned him on, not the lure of the gaming tables, or restaurants which were all about show instead of serving real food. Not for the first time, she wondered what had made him leave Sicily.

She walked towards the shiny black car which was

waiting on the Tarmac, glad she'd insisted on a few days to herself before coming here. She'd told Rocco she needed to organise someone to take her place at the shop and water her plants for her and that much was true, but really she'd needed time to compose herself. To strengthen her resolve not to do anything she might later regret and try to achieve a state of impartiality before she faced her estranged husband again. She'd told herself that whatever happened, she couldn't afford to let desire cloud her judgement and on the plane journey here she'd convinced herself that she had succeeded. But as she looked around in vain for Rocco's dark head and spectacular body, she realised her heart was racing and her skin was clammy—and if *that* wasn't desire then what was?

The uniformed chauffeur stepped forward to open the car door for her.

'Welcome to Monaco, Signora Barberi,' he said in perfect English, with a marked French accent. 'Unfortunately, your husband has been delayed and was unable to meet your flight. He asked me to say he will see you at the house.'

Nicole opened her mouth to tell the driver that she actually preferred to be called Ms Watson these days, until she remembered. *None of this was real.* She wasn't a feisty singleton who was forging a new and independent life for herself. She was supposed to be a woman fighting tooth and nail to hang onto her marriage. So be that woman.

Giving what she hoped was a suitably disappointed expression, she slid onto the back seat of the limousine, pressing her knees together and trying not to think how scruffy the faded denim of her jeans looked against the opulence of the car.

The seat was deliciously soft and the vehicle was coolly air-conditioned, but even so it was difficult to relax. As they drove through the pristine streets of Monaco, Nicole sat as stiffly as someone on their way to a job interview. She'd barely slept a wink since Rocco had turned up at her shop and sent her thoughts and her senses into disarray. Suddenly it hadn't been so easy to put him into that forbidden box where he'd been locked away for so long. Suddenly she'd found herself wondering how on earth she was going to pretend to be reconciling a marriage which had barely got off the ground in the first place. When they'd been nothing but a pair of mismatched strangers with nothing in common other than twin tragedies in their young lives.

They were both orphans: Nicole had been dumped outside a snowy hospital in a shopping bag and Rocco's parents had been killed outright in a speedboat accident when he'd been fourteen. Nicole had thought their dual losses might have provided some kind of bond, but Rocco had adamantly refused to discuss the past. Whenever she'd tried to bring up the subject he would shake his head and tell her it had happened a long time ago and he was over it. And she should be over it, too. He'd told her they should list their blessings instead. She had found herself a kind adoptive mother—and he and his grandfather had helped rear his two heartbroken younger siblings.

They were both over it, he'd insisted.

Nicole stared out of the car window as they passed the fancy stores with designer clothes and jewellery which made you feel you'd been transplanted into the centre of Paris. This was real high-end living, she thought, and once again found it difficult to reconcile Rocco living in such a glitzy place. But what did she really know about him? She was hardly qualified to cast judgement on a man so far out of her league, who had never really allowed her to get close to him. A billionaire who would never have married her if she hadn't been carrying his baby. Nicole felt a brief spear of pain as she pushed her fingers back through her curls. Even now she couldn't believe how two people from opposite ends of the social spectrum should have become lovers—something which had caused outrage at the Barberi family's swanky Mayfair offices, where Nicole been employed as an office cleaner and Rocco was the big boss.

Not that she'd ever intended to be a cleaner. She'd been about to take up a scholarship at one of London's most prestigious art schools when her adoptive mother had been struck down by a virulent form of cancer. Fired by fear and devotion, Nicole had nursed the kindly woman who had taken in the abandoned little girl. The lonely child who had passed through streams of foster parents before Peggy Watson had appeared in her life as a saviour. Nicole hadn't been able to imagine a life without her but, despite her frightened prayers, Peggy had died a painful death. And something in Nicole died along with her.

Grief had left her barely able to lift a paintbrush, let

alone have any ideas worth putting down on paper. Ignoring the pleadings of her teachers, she had deferred her place at art school. Suddenly, she'd felt *old*—as if she'd had nothing in common with the whacky art students and their garish clothes. How could she possibly behave in a carefree way when inside she'd felt so numb? All she'd wanted was a well-paid job she didn't have to think about—and cleaning the Barberi offices had provided the ideal solution. She'd told herself it was just a case of recovering her confidence and clawing together some savings until she felt ready to continue with her art. And that had been her intended path, until the night she'd bumped into the Sicilian billionaire who, against all the odds, had been destined to become her husband.

She'd known who he was because he'd had a reputation for staying late and burning the midnight oil. And like all her co-workers, she'd agreed that the workaholic billionaire was the hunkiest man she'd ever seen. But Nicole had regarded Rocco Barberi in the same way you might regard the leading man in your favourite TV box-set—easy to fantasise about, but totally out of reach. Until the evening they had collided—literally. When Nicole had been carrying her mop and bucket along the corridor and seen the Sicilian heading towards her and they'd been so busy staring at each other that their paths had crossed. The metal bucket had caught the edge of the tycoon's ankle and Nicole had looked down in horror to see soapy water sloshing all over his pristine suit trousers and handmade shoes.

'Oh, my gosh. I'm so sorry,' she'd stumbled, looking up to find herself transfixed by the bluest pair of eyes she'd ever seen. 'I… I wasn't looking where I was going.'

'And neither was I. *Non importa*.' He had made a careless movement with his hand. 'They will clean.'

He'd still been staring at her, staring at her as if he'd known her, or as if he hadn't been able to quite believe what he'd been seeing. And Nicole had felt exactly the same. She might have been a virgin and naïve in the ways of men, but she'd been unable to deny the powerful attraction which had temporarily incapacitated them both. It hadn't seemed to matter that she'd been wearing a blue uniform which had been straining across her breasts, nor that her flyaway curls had been tugged back with a single strand of the green velvet ribbon she always wore, because it matched her eyes. Or that the man in front of her had exuded a power and status which was many lofty rungs above her own. She'd just felt as if she knew him. As if they'd met in a previous life. Or something.

When she'd analysed it afterwards, she'd realised just how dumb she'd been. All that had happened was that she'd been captivated by a man who any painter in a life class would drool over and he had obviously felt something very similar. Their connection had been purely physical. Or chemical. A freak of nature which shouldn't have gone anywhere else, except that it had.

She'd felt apologetic the next day but she'd also felt intensely *alive*—as if he'd woken her from a long sleep. She'd painted him a little postcard—the first time she'd picked up a brush since Peggy's death—and on it she'd depicted a cartoon of Rocco standing in a sea of soapy water on which floated an empty bucket and the single word, *sorry*, at the bottom of the card.

Maybe Rocco had been frustrated at the time and that was why he'd thrown caution to the wind and told her how much the postcard had made him laugh, before asking her out for a drink. And maybe Nicole had just wanted something joyful to happen after the two bleak years since Peggy's death. Either way, their drinks had lain untouched, and the dazzling skyline outside the fancy rooftop bar had gone unnoticed. He'd asked her to dinner and she'd said yes, and it had been the most wonderful evening of her life. But he hadn't touched her, even though she had desperately wanted him to.

A week later they'd had dinner again and then, over a drink following a trip to Milan, he'd asked if she'd ever been on the London Eye. She hadn't as it happened, and as the giant wheel had circled London's imposing monuments Nicole had realised that she was completely smitten by her billionaire boss. Smitten enough to find herself at his apartment later that day with Rocco breaking through her hymen with a groan of hunger followed by disbelief.

Apparently, it was a big thing in Sicily for a man to take a woman's virginity and Rocco had alternately stormed at her, before hugging her tightly to his chest and then lowering his head to suck on her nipples. It had gone on like that for days. Snatched moments of bliss—even at work. That time on the desk would be scorched in her memory for ever. She'd never known that sex could be so *addictive* and Rocco had told her he felt exactly the same.

But then something had changed.

When Rocco had started buying her gradually more daring items of underwear and asking her to wear them Nicole had been eager to try out his sexy commands, yet on some deeper level—she'd been a bit wary, too. Had instinct warned her that the more outrageous his demands, the more he'd seemed to be distancing himself from her? Had he already decided her humble status meant he should end their liaison—and the provocative items of lingerie had been helping highlight her unsuitability? She'd been about to tell him he was making her feel like an object, when she'd missed her period, and her newly tender breasts had told her what the pregnancy test had quickly confirmed—that she was carrying Rocco Barberi's baby.

Telling him had been nothing like the rose-tinted version she'd secretly longed for—a version as far away as possible from her own bleak beginnings on the snowy steps of a wintry hospital. She'd wanted to give him the news somewhere neutral, but he'd told her he was expecting a call and maybe they should take a rain check on the date they'd planned—and had he mentioned that he was planning a trip to the States the following week and wouldn't be around for some time? And that was when it had all come blurting out, there in his penthouse office—with her untouched mop and bucket standing on the floor beside her feet.

'Rocco, I'm pregnant.'

She would never forget his expression as he'd looked

up from his computer. A brief shuttering followed by a shadowed caution.

'You're certain?'

'Positive.'

'And it's…'

His words had faded but a sudden chill had washed over Nicole's skin.

'Yours?' she'd questioned with a perception which had made her suddenly feel quite sick. 'Is that what you were going to say, Rocco?'

He had shaken his head. 'Of course not.'

She hadn't believed him and had started to cry when he'd 'jokingly' suggested she might have deliberately sabotaged the condom in order to trap him. Had her woeful, red-eyed face tugged at his conscience? Was that why he'd risen from his desk and walked across the office towards her? His unkind words had been blotted out by the deep sense of gratitude she'd felt when he'd taken her in his arms and told her that of course she must marry him. He was going to stand by her and that meant a lot to someone who had been abandoned as a baby. And of course, she had thought herself in love with him. Yet all the time she had been acutely aware of the dutiful way he went about preparing for their marriage—as if he was being forced into something he'd never intended.

If she'd been an independent woman instead of a broke cleaner with hardly any qualifications, might her answer have been different? Would she have tried to go it alone to bring up her baby and told him he was very welcome to have access visits whenever he wanted? She thought not. Even if she *had* been inclined to embrace single parenthood, she recognised that Rocco would never have allowed that to happen. She had been carrying *his* child and therefore she had been *his* possession. That was something else she understood. It was something to do with being Sicilian and something to do with being a Barberi.

Their unlikely union had excited a flurry of interest in the European gossip but the Cinderella slant of the newspaper articles had made her feel somehow...*less than*—and that wasn't a good way to start a marriage. And anyway—the whole thing had been a waste of time, hadn't it? Rocco had only gone through with the wedding because she'd been pregnant—but her body had been unable to hold onto the baby she'd wanted so much. She had failed the baby, just as she had failed Rocco. She had let everyone down. She felt the sting of tears at the backs of her eyes and dabbed at them furiously with a curled-up fist.

She wasn't going to think about that.

She wasn't going to let herself go there.

But Nicole's hands were trembling as the powerful car suddenly turned off the main drag and began to ascend a steep and curving street before eventually coming to a halt at the top, outside a deep rose-hued house with its amazing view over Monaco's harbour. She looked up at it in surprise. Somehow she hadn't imagined Rocco living somewhere like this—in a house on a street—not when he had grown up amid roaming acres of olive groves and vineyards in beautiful rural Sicily.

The front door was opened immediately, almost as if

someone had been watching out for the car. But it wasn't Rocco who stood on the doorstep, but a chic woman in a black and white uniform, which made Nicole realise why so many women wore French maid outfits to fancy-dress parties when they were trying to look sexy.

'Welcome, *signora*,' the woman said, with a coral-tinted smile. 'I'm Veronique and I'm the housekeeper. Signor Barberi's assistant, Michele, is waiting upstairs for you in his office and I will take you there.'

Slightly disorientated by the size of the entrance hall, Nicole turned to stare out of the still-open front door where the limousine was parked. 'But my suitcase—'

'The driver will bring it in and leave it in your room,' said Veronique. 'Do not concern yourself. Please. Come with me.'

Nicole followed the housekeeper along a gleaming marble corridor and into a huge room whose only concessions to being an office were a giant desk and a row of clocks on the wall depicting different time zones around the world. For the most part it just looked like an amazing room with an equally amazing view. A tall blonde was waiting for them, her high-heeled shoes matching her fitted pink dress, and Nicole wondered just how many beautiful women Rocco surrounded himself with and whether any of them provided any additional extras.

But that's none of your business, she told herself fiercely trying to downplay the savage little kick of jealousy which flared up inside her. If he wants to sleep with the staff, that's up to him.

The blonde stepped forward and extended her hand.

'Hi! I'm Michele, Rocco's assistant, and I'm delighted to be able to welcome you to Monaco, Signora Barberi.'

'Please—call me Nicole.'

Michele smiled. 'Nicole it is. I'm afraid he's a bit tied up at the moment.' She gave an apologetic shrug which suggested she was no stranger to conveying this message. 'His last meeting went on longer than anticipated and he's taking a conference call right now. He said to tell you he'll be with you as soon as he can and that I should show you around.'

Unsure if Rocco's assistant was aware of the make-believe nature of their reconciliation, Nicole forced herself to adopt an expression of lively curiosity. 'That would be great.'

'So why don't we start down here?'

Nicole followed Rocco's shapely assistant through the most luxurious house she had ever seen. High-ceilinged reception rooms were studded with modern furniture and once again, she couldn't help comparing it to Rocco's Sicilian home. There was no dark wood, or furniture which had been worn down by previous generations who were now unsmiling faces in framed sepia photographs. Everything looked so new and so…bright. She found herself liking it because it had no obvious history and an unexpected smile curved the edges of her mouth. A bit like her, really.

Briefly, she looked around the well-stocked library, peered into an imposing gym and gazed wistfully at the infinity pool which overlooked the Mediterranean, wishing she'd remembered to bring a swimsuit. There were six bedrooms in all, the largest of which was obviously Rocco's, and Nicole's heart flipped when she saw *her* suitcase sitting in the centre of the floor.

'And this is the master suite,' Michele was saying. 'I think you'll find everything you need, but please let me know if there's anything else I can get you. The fundraiser doesn't start until eight tonight so you have plenty of time to acclimatise yourself. Would you like me to leave you to unpack? I expect you want to hang up your dresses.' Michele glanced diplomatically at Nicole's battered little suitcase as she indicated a section of inbuilt wardrobe doors. 'Rocco has left plenty of space for your belongings. Or perhaps you would rather have something to drink first?'

Nicole wasn't planning on putting her belongings anywhere near Rocco's, but she didn't want to embarrass his assistant by telling her that. And there was no way she could ever sleep in here—it was too unsettling on too many levels. She could sense Rocco's presence everywhere. That tantalising scent which was all his—a subtle mix of sandalwood and bergamot. The well-thumbed crime novel which lay open on the bedside table which was probably on exactly the same page as it had been since his last holiday. She could see a pair of gold and lapis lazuli cufflinks lying on the dressing table—and the intimacy of being inside his bedroom again was causing her heart to contract with a flurry of emotions which was making her feel dizzy.

'Actually, I'd love something to drink,' she said weakly.

'In that case, come and I'll have someone bring it up

to the terrace, which I think you might like.' Michele's smile widened. 'You see, I saved the best for last.'

As soon as Nicole stepped out onto the terrace she realised Michele hadn't been exaggerating. Pursing her lips into a silent whistle of appreciation, she looked out over the balcony. This was the kind of view which only wads of money could buy and Nicole's first thought was how much she would like to recreate these colours on clay. The deep azure of the sea lay before her in an endless dazzle and above it was the paler hue of the sky. How incredible it would be to make a collection in all these different shades of blue and maybe to hint at the greens and greys of the distant mountains. It was opulent and stunning and it felt unreal. In fact, *she* felt unreal. But hadn't she always felt out of place in this wealthy world she'd left behind?

'Would you like water, or tea?' Michele was asking. 'Or we have champagne, if you prefer.'

Nicole shook her head. 'No, honestly. Water would be perfect. Thanks.'

After Michele had gone, Nicole leaned over the railings and gazed ahead but this time she wasn't really focussing on the view. She thought about the child she'd once been—the insecure little outcast who had been pushed from pillar to post until Peggy Watson had taken her in. Could that orphaned little girl ever have imagined standing somewhere like this, about to draw a line under her marriage? And despite everything, she felt a pang of pain that she hadn't been able to make it work. It made her start wondering if there had been anything she could have done to have saved it. If her own grief had made her keep Rocco at arm's length. Perhaps it had. Perhaps she might handle it very differently now.

But you can't keep going back over the past. It's too late to do anything about it now. It's over.

'Beautiful, isn't it?' A rich voice washed over her skin like dark silk and Nicole turned round, her heart clenching. Because Rocco was walking towards her, a glass in his hand-the darkness of his hair almost blue-black in the bright sunshine.

'Very beautiful,' she said breathlessly.

'That's Cap Ferrat directly opposite—and the land you can see over there is Italy.' He moved directly in front of her and held out the glass. 'I believe you told Michele you wanted something to drink.'

Nicole's heart was pounding and suddenly her senses were going crazy because she couldn't seem to think straight when he was standing this close. Her body seemed programmed to react in a way she couldn't prevent—no matter how hard she tried. For a split-second she wanted to put her arms around his neck. To melt into the hardness of his body while he began to stroke her in that way which had always made her shiver with longing…

Until she forced herself to remember that this was Rocco. Heartless Rocco who didn't give a damn about her. Who had ridden roughshod over her feelings and brought her out here to help further his ruthless business ambitions. With a tight smile she took the water from him and sipped from the crystal glass. 'Thanks,' she said.

'You're welcome.' His blue eyes were mocking. 'Made yourself at home?'

'Easier said than done,' she quipped. 'This place is so big it reminds me of one of those stately homes in London. I suppose if your business deal falls through you could always charge an entrance fee and make a little extra money on the side.'

'A novel suggestion,' he murmured.

'I'm nothing if not enterprising, Rocco. And I've been running my own shop for the past year so I'm pretty much up to speed with running a small business.'

Reluctantly, Rocco smiled. He'd forgotten that her very different upbringing gave her a sometimes irreverent take on his world, and how it had once enchanted him. Just as he'd forgotten how fresh and vibrant she could look, without even trying. He narrowed his eyes. Compared to the manufactured glamour of most of the women he mixed with, her natural beauty seemed to shine through—and the suddenly powerful throb of his groin was an indication of just how instinctively his body responded to that.

'Did Michele show you where everything was?' he questioned unevenly.

'She did.' She put the glass down. 'Though I thought you might have turned up at the airport to meet me.'

'And were you disappointed?'

She shrugged. 'I don't know that I would describe it as *disappointment*. I just thought that after all the fuss you made about me coming out here, you might have made the effort to meet me from the plane. If you're supposed to be playing the spouse eager to get his marriage back on track, ignoring my arrival isn't really the way to go about it.'

'I'd planned to be there but I'm afraid it didn't work out that way,' he said smoothly. 'I was snowed under with work.'

'So I gather.'

Her thick curls were gleaming darkly in the bright sunshine and suddenly Rocco found himself wanting to tangle his fingers in them, the way he used to do. 'What can I say?' he said, with a shrug. 'It was a call I needed to take.'

'But mightn't it have occurred to you to postpone it?' she continued coolly. 'Rather than dumping me on your assistant, who clearly isn't quite sure what to do with me?'

'Nobody was dumping you, Nicole. It was urgent.'

'It's always urgent with you, isn't it, Rocco? Work always takes precedence.'

He raised his eyebrows. 'You think organisations like the Barberi Foundation just run themselves?'

'No, I don't think that. But I do think work can become an addiction and a substitute.'

'A substitute for what?'

'You tell me. When was the last time you had a holiday?'

'You know I don't like holidays.' He frowned. 'Anyway, what difference does it make who shows you around?'

And that was the trouble, Nicole reminded herself. He really couldn't see it. He had no understanding of the way he treated the people in his life—as if they were mere accessories, to be brought out if and when it suited him. Wasn't it time someone told him? Pointed out a few home-truths which were long overdue? She pushed back her curls, aware that she might be about to become the cliché of a nagging wife—but also aware there were things she'd never dared say to him while they'd been together and maybe she had nothing to lose now. 'Didn't you think it might have been awkward for me when your assistant mistakenly assumed we'd be sharing a bedroom?'

'That was no mistake, *tesoro*,' he said softly. 'We're supposed to be giving our marriage another go and naturally we will need to share a bedroom.'

She shook her head. 'But that's where you're wrong. It's only a game, Rocco,' she reminded him. 'Remember?'

It was only a game, Rocco repeated to himself silently—but right then it was hard to think of anything other than how much he desired her, despite the cheap jewellery and faded jeans. She was far more assertive than she'd ever been in the past and this unaccustomed display of spirit from his once passive wife was doing peculiar things to his pulse-rate. He swallowed. He thought about other women he had dated before his marriage. Classy women, who wore designer clothes instead of jeans and a shirt. With subtle diamonds glinting in their earlobes, not big silver hoops which dangled amid the wild tangle of curls.

Yet Nicole was the one who did it for him. Still did, if he was being honest. Who powered his heart so that it hammered against his chest like a piston. Who made him feel about sixteen again. Rocco felt a sudden rush of lust which wiped out every thought other than the blindingly obvious. He thought about the way her body convulsed and spasmed around him when she was coming—and the erection which was currently throbbing hotly at his groin became almost unbearable.

Sucking in a deep breath, he tried to assert the self-control which had become his default at the age of fourteen, when he had been forced to grow up overnight, but for once it was proving elusive. Was she feeling it too—this attraction which was almost tangible as it sizzled in the air around them? He looked into her eyes as all kinds of new possibilities began to open up in his mind. 'It may only be a game,' he stated softly, 'but I think we need to make it as convincing a game as possible, don't you?'

'Not by sharing a space,' she argued. 'And before you try telling me that your staff will notice we're not in the same room—I don't care. I'm assuming everyone who works for you is loyal, since loyalty is something you've always demanded from the people around you.'

'And were you loyal to me, Nicole?' he said suddenly.

The question took her by surprise. 'Yes, I was. Completely. More than you'll ever know. 'She gave a short laugh. 'Or maybe you aren't aware of the offers I got to tell my story when our marriage broke down?'

He leaned back against the railing and studied her, his blue eyes thoughtful. 'What kind of offers?'

She shrugged. 'Oh, you know. Big ones. Journalists who tracked me down wondering why a Barberi ex-wife was living such a shabby existence when she'd been married to one of the richest men on the planet. Why I was working in a puny little art shop instead of living in a luxury flat and giving your credit card a battering. I don't know why you're looking so surprised, Rocco—you can see how much they might have wanted the story. Isn't that what newspaper readers love to read about? The fairy-tale marriage which came to such an abrupt ending.'

His sapphire eyes had become shuttered by the thick curtain of his dark lashes. 'But you didn't talk to them?'

'Of course I didn't.' Frustratedly, Nicole shook her head. How could he even *ask* that? The raw pain of losing their baby had been replaced by a kind of numbness that her marriage was over—they had pushed each other so far away that there was nothing left between them. She'd forced herself into a zombified state of acceptance as she had stumbled through the days without realising what was going on, only knowing she needed to start over. She'd convinced herself that Sicily had been nothing but a strange interlude and she needed to reconnect with England, but it hadn't been easy. She'd felt like a tiny craft thrown into a raging sea, not knowing which direction life would take her. One minute she'd been a cleaner and then a billionaire's wife. One minute a mother-to-be and the next…nothing. There was no word in the English language to describe a mother who had lost her child, was there? Nicole swallowed. Only someone who was seriously deluded would have wanted to relive that pain and disruption and see it printed in a newspaper. 'Did you really think I would ever talk to a journalist?' she demanded. 'Did you?'

He shrugged as his mouth flattened into its habitual uncompromising line. 'The financial rewards might have tempted some people.'

'But I'm not *some people*, Rocco! When will you ever believe that I was never interested in the money? That wasn't what attracted me to you. What you've never had—you never miss.'

He was still studying her, still with that same intense scrutiny. 'Is that why you left without taking anything?'

Nicole hesitated. Maybe this was what it all boiled down to for him. Because for Rocco, everyone had their price, didn't they? He'd told her about the women who had been bewitched by the Barberi fortune and were eager to get themselves a slice of it for themselves. Just as he'd told her about the people who tried to muscle in when they found out who he was. He didn't really trust people and never let them close. Much easier for him to believe that everyone had an ulterior motive where he was concerned because that gave him a legitimate reason to keep people at a distance. She wondered how honest she could afford to be—yet surely it was a waste of time trying to conceal the truth from him now, in these dying days of their relationship. Because her answers were academic. Whatever Rocco wanted, it wasn't her.

She stared at him. 'I didn't take anything because I wanted to cut all ties between us. In fact, I never wanted to see you again.'

She met his eyes with a steady challenge and Rocco stilled. How *dared* she be so dismissive? It was an insult to his pride, yes—but it struck at something darker, too. Something deep inside which made him want to lash out at her blatant rejection. Yet there was no need to fight, not when there were different ways for him to vent his frustration or show her just what a mistake she had made. Things which had been on his mind all day—all week—ever since he'd walked into her little art shop in Cornwall and seen her bite her lip so that it took on a deep, rosy glow. And despite having told himself this was not going to happen, he found himself taking a step towards her.

'So you never wanted to see me again?' he mused silkily. 'In which case it didn't work very well for you, did it? Seeing as you're here with me now.'

She continued to hold his gaze with a look of pure defiance. 'And I can walk away whenever I choose,' she said. 'Divorce or no divorce. Either you accept that I'm not sharing a room with you, or I'm out of here. Because I'm not interested in you that way, Rocco, if that's what you're thinking.'

'You're saying you don't want to have sex with me?'

She nodded. 'That's exactly what I'm saying.'

He saw her green eyes widen as he reached out to pull her into his arms, her luscious curves instantly pliable beneath his fingers. 'Then perhaps you'd like to put that to the test, my defiant wife,' he murmured as he lowered his head towards hers.

CHAPTER FOUR

HE WAS GOING to kiss her and after everything she'd just said, Nicole knew she needed to stop him . But suddenly she found herself governed by a much deeper need than preserving her sanity, or her pride. A need and a hunger which swept over her with the speed of a bush fire. As Rocco's shadowed face lowered towards her she found past and present fusing, so that for a disconcerting moment she forgot everything except the urgent hunger in her body. Because hadn't her Sicilian husband always been able to do this—to captivate her with the lightest touch and to tantalise her with that smouldering look of promise? And hadn't there been many nights since they'd separated when she'd woken up, still half fuddled with sleep, and found herself yearning for the taste of his lips on hers just one more time? And now she had it.

One more time.

She opened her mouth and Rocco used the opportunity to fasten his mouth over hers in the most perfects of fits. And instantly Nicole felt helpless—caught up in the powerful snare of a sexual mastery which wiped out everything else. She gave a moan of pleasure because it had been so long since she had done this. She'd forgotten what it was like to kiss him because kissing was one of the first casualties of a failing marriage. You stopped kissing and touching and all too soon it was difficult to contemplate anything other than the icy barrier you had created between you.

And Nicole had felt like a living statue since they'd been apart. As if she were made from marble. As if the flesh and blood part of her were some kind of half-forgotten dream. Slowly but surely she had withdrawn from the sensual side of her nature until she'd convinced herself she was dead and unfeeling inside. But here came Rocco to wake her dormant sexuality with nothing more than a single kiss. It was like some stupid fairy story. It was scary and powerful. She didn't *want* to want him, and yet...

She wanted him.

Her lips opened wider as his tongue slid inside her mouth—eagerly granting him that early intimacy as if preparing the way for another. She began to shiver as his hands started to explore her—rediscovering her body with an impatient hunger, as if it were the first time he'd ever touched her. His fingers skated over her breasts, palms massaging the swollen contours until each taut and aching nipple was in an exquisite state of arousal. Instinctively she writhed against him and felt the hard cradle of his desire. And now the moaning sound she could hear was *his* as he deepened the kiss—underpinning it with a sudden sense of urgency.

'Nicole,' he said unevenly and she'd never heard him say her name like that before.

Her arms were locked behind his neck as again he circled his hips against hers in unmistakable invitation and, somewhere in the back of her mind, Nicole could hear the small voice of reason imploring her to take control of the situation. It was urging her to call a halt to what they were doing and to do it now, before it was too late. But once again she ignored it. Against the powerful tide of passion, that little voice was drowned out and she allowed pleasure to shimmer over her skin.

She drew back a little to pull some air into her lungs—and the expression on his face both shocked and thrilled her. Because she'd never seen Rocco look like this before. The tension had turned his features into a taut mask. His eyes were blackened with lust, their sapphire brilliance almost concealed by the dilated pupils. Two lines of colour flared along the edges of his high cheekbones and contrasted with the hue of his olive skin.

'So, *tesoro*.' His murmured words were provocative as his circling groin gave yet another candid demonstration of just how aroused he was. 'Is this what you've been missing?'

Nicole swallowed. She should tell him not to be so arrogant. She should tell him a lot of things which were long overdue. But she was in no fit state to give a coherent answer because he was idly whispering his middle finger down over her midriff and somehow the barrier of her filmy shirt was making what was happening doubly provocative. So that instead of telling him to stop, she found herself whispering, 'Yes.'

He gave a little groan of satisfaction as he slid his

hand up beneath her shirt to cup the breast which was straining madly against her bra. So close to the skin, she thought frustratedly—and yet much too far away. Her mouth dried as he began to circle a nipple with his thumb and her eyelids fluttered to a close as she felt it puckering beneath the lace. How could a touch which was barely there feel so *incredible*? 'Oh,' she said, her voice sounding slurred against the seeking pressure of his kiss.

He gave a low laugh as his hand moved from her breast down to the waistband of her jeans and Nicole held her breath. Would he dare go further? Surely she shouldn't allow *this*? She knew she ought to break the spell yet she was so in thrall to what was happening that she was powerless to move. She heard the rasp of her zip as he began to slide it down and she held her breath, praying he would continue even though she knew he ought to stop. And now he was slipping his hand into the space provided by the open denim, and was easing one finger on a downward path over the warm surface of her belly. She swallowed.

'Is there something else you would prefer me to do?' he murmured. 'In which case, you'd better tell me, because although I have many skills where women are concerned, I'm afraid mind-reading isn't one of them.'

His teasing incited her—it made the heat raging inside her intensify to such a pitch that the idea of calling a halt to this madness seemed unbearable. Yet it angered her, too. How dared he bring up the subject of *other women* at a time like this? Did he think she didn't care about stuff like that? With a yelp of rage she kissed him hard and she could feel his mouth curving into a smile, because by now he was slipping his fingers inside her panties. And didn't the molten wetness he encountered there seem like a kind of betrayal? A physical demonstration of just how much she still wanted him, no matter how much she wished she didn't. Her head fell back as he began to circle the tip of her clitoris with a feather-light touch.

'Oh, my,' he said softly as she quivered uncontrollably beneath the rhythmic caress of his finger. He gave a soft laugh. 'Oh, Nicole. Just like old times. So wet and so *hot*. I think we'd better do something about this, hadn't we, *mio tesoro*?'

She opened her mouth to tell him he'd got it all wrong but her desire was so great that she couldn't speak. And even if she could, what the hell could she say?

Stop what you're doing because it's wrong. It's making me feel weak and vulnerable and I vowed never to let myself feel that way again.

Because right now she didn't care about any of that. All she cared about was the way he was making her feel. So she stayed silent as layer upon layer of pleasure began to build—so sweet and so achingly familiar. It took her to such a pitch of sexual hunger that she found herself wanting to whisper his name over and over again, like some life-affirming mantra. She was going to come—she knew she was—when the sudden memory of his mocking words crashed into her mind and shattered the magic spell he was weaving.

Just like old times, he'd said.

But it wasn't, was it? It was nothing like old times,

when she'd still been naïve and foolish enough to think there was some connection between them, which could get deeper if they worked on it. They weren't those star-crossed lovers she'd imagined them to be and nor were they the unlikely newlyweds with no idea how to communicate with each other. The past was gone and this was not how she intended her future to be.

Nicole clamped her hand over Rocco's wrist, halting the finger still poised with tantalising precision over the engorged bud as she summoned up all the willpower she possessed. And although her body was screaming out its objections, she blocked them. Because she'd been through a lot to get to where she was today. She'd worked hard and built her little business up from scratch—and it might not be very much, but it was all *hers*. She was beginning to establish herself as the artist she'd always wanted to be before life and Rocco had sucked her up and wrung her out to dry. She'd even started to convince herself that one day she would be properly over him. Was she really prepared to jeopardise everything—including her precious self-respect—just because her hormones had been reactivated by Rocco Barberi's overt sexuality?

Heart pounding, she yanked his hand out of her panties and stepped away to turn her back on him while she readjusted her clothing. Her cheeks were burning as she zipped up her jeans and smoothed down her white shirt while the silver chains around her neck jangled like wind chimes. Slowly she came back to reality, blinking as she took in her surroundings to realise that they'd been making out on a penthouse terrace not far from

Monaco's picture-book harbour. And while they weren't exactly being overlooked, what was to stop someone on one of those fancy yachts from peering through a pair of binoculars and seeing them? Some paparazzi photographer taking a few candid snaps to earn himself some unexpected money? Or one of Rocco's staff turning up with papers for him to sign? She gave a violent shudder of remorse as she turned on him.

'How dare you try to have sex with me?' she hissed.

Unabashed, he shrugged. 'That isn't the message I was just getting. And isn't it a little late in the day for such an outraged reaction? I thought only teenagers played games like that.'

'I wasn't *playing games*!'

'Letting me go only so far and no further?' He raised his eyebrows. 'You don't consider that an adolescent game?'

'Not in the circumstances, no. You were making me feel like...like an *object*.'

'I was making you feel pleasure,' he corrected. 'What's wrong with that?'

She shook her head. 'And now you're insulting me by asking such a dumb question. Having sex with you would complicate an already complicated situation—we both know that. And that's not the reason I'm here.'

'But you wanted me,' he said slowly, his bright sapphire gaze taking in the breasts which were still heaving beneath her filmy shirt. 'You want me now. Your body is crying out for me to touch you again. Surely even you wouldn't deny that, Nicole.'

Nicole bit her lip, angry that he could look so cool

and controlled when she felt so hot and bothered. Hating the fact that if she denied his accusation, she could rightly be accused of hypocrisy. And she didn't *have* to answer him. She could flounce off this terrace any time she wanted except that wouldn't be a very mature response, and she was supposed to be all about maturity these days. Wasn't that one of the benefits of getting older, that you learnt from the knocks you experienced along the way? You learnt that what didn't kill you made you stronger, even if at the time you wanted to just curl up and die.

She smoothed her hands down over her ruffled curls in a vain attempt to smooth them. 'Of course I *want* you,' she said carefully. 'Or rather, my body does. You are a very charismatic man, as I'm sure many women must have told you in the past—'

'You were always one of the most vociferous advocates,' he reminded her softly.

'I know. But I was young. And I don't think talking about the way we felt back then is particularly helpful,' she said. Because she was starting to realise how dangerous it could be. It was feeding those feelings she'd forced herself to repress. Dangerous feelings about love and longing, which had been pointless then and were even more pointless now.

'Let's just chalk it up to experience,' she continued, swallowing down the lump in her throat. 'We were just two people trying to do the right thing. It just didn't work out.'

A thoughtful look shadowed his face. 'But there's no reason why that should stop us having sex right now, since it's what we both want,' he murmured. 'Isn't that so?'

Nicole shook her head, trying to fight the sudden desire provoked by the velvety caress of his words. 'That's not going to happen, Rocco.'

'Do you want to tell me why?'

'You know why. Because it would feel…wrong. And I'm pretty certain it would invalidate our two years of separation and take even longer to get a divorce.'

'Ah, yes. Your precious divorce,' he mused.

'My ticket to freedom, you mean? Yours, too.'

His smile was mocking. 'At least you've answered one question for me,' he observed.

She looked at him. 'Oh? What question is that?'

'Back in England, I asked if there was another man waiting in the wings and you didn't give me a satisfactory answer. But now I'd be prepared to bet my entire fortune there isn't.'

'I thought you said mind-reading wasn't one of your skills.'

'It's not. It doesn't need to be. It's written all over your face, Nicole.'

'What is?' she said, even though on some level she was aware she might be walking straight into a trap.

'You're so horny,' he answered throatily. 'Hornier than any woman would be if she'd been having sex on a regular basis. Yet you were able to pull back, despite being so close to coming. Such steely resolve.' He gave a soft laugh. 'And I admire that quality in you, Nicole— even if I'm the one who ultimately missed out.'

His words wrong-footed her because they sounded

like a compliment and just like the next woman, Nicole was a sucker for a compliment. Had he said it to lull her into a false sense of complacency before moving in for the big seduction? She wondered how many other women had stood here, like this, their clothes all rumpled and their blood pulsing as they went willingly to the Sicilian billionaire's bed. Well, she wasn't going to be one of them.

'I'm ending this conversation as of now,' she said. 'And now I need to find myself a separate bedroom because this is a *pretend* reconciliation, not a real one. We don't share rooms and we don't make out.'

Rocco saw the determined way she pulled back her shoulders and recognised she was serious. A flicker of disquiet edged his growing frustration. If it had been any other woman he could have persuaded her with a kiss. A kiss which this time she would find impossible to stop, because if Rocco Barberi was hell-bent on something, or someone, he always got it. But the steadfast expression flattening his estranged wife's soft lips was unfamiliar and suddenly he realised he didn't know this new Nicole at all.

When he'd gone to see her in England sex had been the last thing on his mind. He'd gone there to punish her and to use her, not to make love to her, yet something had changed his mind. That kiss they'd just shared had started out as nothing more than a challenge—a demonstration of his own power in the light of her resistance—and yet she had responded in a way which had sent his desire soaring.

And yet she had pushed him away.

His heart pounded, because now he was determined to have her one last time and nothing was going to stop him. But for once he realised that he was going to have to work for it. Maybe he should give her enough space to realise what she was missing, instead of pushing his own agenda. How long before she decided that denying her hunger for him was simply not sustainable—and slipped into his arms again?

So he nodded his head and gave her a cool smile. 'If that's what you want, then that's what you shall have. Take any bedroom you want—there are plenty to choose from,' he said, enjoying the confusion which had suddenly clouded her emerald eyes. 'Just make sure you're ready for the screening and dinner tonight. The car will be here just before eight.'

He ran his gaze over the unruly dark curls and the mismatched silver necklaces and a rogue glimmer of amusement found its way into his voice. 'No doubt you've brought something deeply unsuitable to wear?'

Unexpectedly, her eyes danced in response. 'You think I'm going to turn up looking like this?'

He shrugged. 'I have no idea. I offered to buy you some suitable clothes for this trip but you turned down my offer.'

'Because we tried that once before and it didn't work. Remember? You were so eager to make me into what you thought a Barberi wife should be that I felt like some kind of dress-up doll.'

He frowned. 'I was trying to make you feel more comfortable.'

'What, by employing that expensive stylist who put

me in those horrible starchy dresses which didn't suit me? Or the fancy hairdresser who decided to chop off all my hair so I ended up looking like a shorn lion?'

'That *was* a mistake,' he conceded.

She looked at him uncertainly, clearly taken aback by what for him almost passed as an apology, and the fleeting vulnerability on her face stirred something deep inside him, reminding him what had attracted him to her in the first place. Well, that and her killer body.

'But not any more. Tonight I'm going to wear my hair and clothes exactly as I like them,' she continued airily. 'And if you're worried I'm going to disgrace you with my appearance, Rocco—you shouldn't be.'

'Oh?' He was curious now.

'If people criticise my less than conventional appearance at least it will reinforce why our last-minute attempt at reconciliation didn't work. If they see us together and think "chalk and cheese", they'll wonder why we ever got married in the first place.' She slanted him a challenging look. 'Because although opposites attract—they can also repel. We both know that.'

With that she turned her back on him and left the terrace with a sway of her denim-covered bottom, which Rocco found almost unbearably provocative.

And after she'd gone, he felt restless—a feeling kick-started by the echo of her final words. *Were* they better off without each other? Not right now they weren't. The fingertip he ran over his dry lips only added to his frustration as he breathed in the earthy aroma of her sex. By now she should have been in his bed—eagerly opening her legs so they could lose themselves in sweet oblivion, not leaving him here aching and frustrated.

Looking out to sea, he scowled. When his PA had called to say Nicole had arrived at his Monaco home he had been unprepared for the primitive rush of satisfaction he'd experienced, knowing she was here. Back in the marriage she had walked away from. It had never happened to him before—a woman telling him she was going, and meaning it. Only the stark note lying on top of an unmade bed had made clear her wishes.

Please don't follow me, or try to contact me. It's better this way, Rocco. I'm sorry.

And that had been it. A few words signalling the end. Yet he hadn't seen it coming and shock was something he didn't handle well. Maybe the only thing he didn't handle well—not surprising given his history. He remembered the blood draining from his face as he'd crumpled the note in his fist and had proceeded to do something completely alien. Taking himself off to the bar in the nearby village, he had got himself very, very drunk. Groups of the local Sicilian men had looked surprised because Rocco Barberi was not known as a drinker. He remembered smashing his fist down hard on the counter and shattering a glass and hearing the old men's voices raised in alarm. Someone must have made a phone call because he vaguely recalled his oldest friend arriving and getting him back to the complex, and Salvatore telling him that women were capricious creatures and she would be back before he knew it.

But she hadn't come back and Rocco had told himself he didn't *want* her back. Why would he want a wife who had deserted him—who had given up at the first hurdle? Yet despite her behaviour, his sense of duty went deep and his tenacity even deeper. He didn't like failure and a shattered marriage fell very firmly into that category. So he had written to her, reminding her of the solemn vows they had made in church and suggesting they give their marriage another go.

She hadn't even bothered to reply and Rocco had geared himself up to resist the demands for money he was certain would follow. He remembered his growing anticipation of the forthcoming battle—a battle he would certainly win—and his determination to bring her to her knees in court. It was the first moment of pleasure he had experienced in a long time. If she wanted his money then she was damned well going to have to fight him for it.

But...*niente*.

Nothing.

There had been no demands for alimony. Even the recent letter from her lawyers had simply requested that the marriage be formally ended. She had asked for nothing and somehow that had only intensified his rage.

His features were set as he undressed and stepped into the shower, but the powerful jets of cold water did little to ease his aching body as he pictured Nicole on the balcony, her rosy lips parted with pleasure as his fingers flicked over her heated flesh and brought her so tantalisingly close to orgasm.

As he towelled the icy droplets from his skin a renewed determination crept over him.

He would have her, he vowed silently as he willed his erection to subside. Because sex was the only thing which would rid him of her enduring memory.

And he would not wait much longer.

CHAPTER FIVE

'So. How do I look? Does my appearance confirm your worst fears, Rocco, or will I pass the test?'

Nicole kept her words deliberately light as she walked into the vast sitting room where Rocco was standing with his back to her, staring through the open windows which overlooked the sea. Because what she was *not* going to do was beat herself up or crumple with shame when she allowed herself to remember how nearly she had succumbed to him earlier. It had happened. She hadn't been expecting it to happen because she'd thought those kind of feelings had left her. But they hadn't, had they? Rocco had melted the icy wall which had surrounded her for so long, and her image of herself as someone who could no longer feel desire had been shattered. Heart pounding, she had left him on the terrace and gone to find herself a bedroom in this vast house of his—glad to escape from his disturbing proximity. But she had lain down on the bed for a long time afterwards, her body trembling with frustrated desire, unable to get him out of her mind.

She let her gaze drift over him, wishing she could

acquire some kind of immunity against him. Dressed in an immaculate dinner suit, his powerful body was silhouetted against the bright light of the Mediterranean but at the sound of her voice he turned round. And even though she tried to fight it, the brief, unguarded expression on his face filled her with pleasure. She'd seen that look of appreciation before—but usually when she was naked. Not when she was wearing a long dress which, apart from a scooped neck and bare arms, covered her body all the way down to her ankles. Fashioned from fine, black jersey it clung to her curves like a second skin and she had teamed it with black pumps and a black bag onto which she'd sewn lots of glittery sequins. The green of the sequins matched her dramatic green necklace and chandelier earrings, which gleamed whenever her wavy hair swayed.

His eyes narrowed as, slowly, they took in her appearance. 'What happened?' he questioned softly. 'Did you rob a bank?'

'I bought this dress from a market stall, as it happens.'

'I wasn't talking about the dress,' he growled. 'I meant the jewels.'

It was a small victory and Nicole couldn't quite hold back her smile of triumph. 'These? They're fake, Rocco. Paste,' she added. 'I told you—nobody can tell the difference these days. And these were cheap enough for it not to matter if I lose one of the stones—not like the time that big diamond fell out of the bracelet you gave me on our wedding day and caused so much trouble with everyone having to hunt round for it.' She was aware that she had started to babble, but maybe that was something to do with the fact that he was still looking at her as a lion might look at a lump of flesh, just before devouring it. And even worse—that she *liked* him looking at her like that. In her current state of frustrated arousal she could have let him look at her like that all day. She resumed her inane monologue about the wedding bracelet. 'Still, at least we were able to get the money back on the insurance and I—'

'Was that why you left behind all the jewellery I gave you?' he interrupted suddenly. 'Because you didn't like it?

There was a short silence and she shrugged her shoulders. 'It was a joint asset,' she said. 'And as such, wasn't really mine to take. And I wanted...'

'What did you want, Nicole?'

She met his gaze, uneasy at this sudden line of questioning from a man who had never cared about such things before. 'A clean break, I think they call it.'

'A clean break,' he echoed, his mouth twisting into a bitter smile. 'Yes, of course. The modern, disposable marriage. If you try hard enough you can pretend it never happened.'

She opened her mouth to ask him what *he* had done to help save it but the sudden pain spearing through her made the words die in her throat. It didn't matter what either of them had done or failed to do. Bottom line was that they'd messed up so and it still had the power to hurt. 'Why rake up all this now, Rocco?' she questioned, trying hard to keep her voice steady. 'I thought the whole idea was for us to appear tonight as a couple who are trying to get it together—and we won't convince anyone if we've been fighting. People can always tell if a couple have been rowing. So why don't you tell me about what kind of event it is, so I can be fully briefed?'

For a moment Rocco didn't answer, unwilling to be placated by this newly assertive Nicole who looked so damned gorgeous that all he wanted to do was to pull her into his arms and get intimate with her, despite the market dress and fake jewels. But maybe she was right. What was the point of sparring when they had a whole evening to get through—a necessary preliminary before he got down to the more important business of seducing her. And when he seduced her... His mouth hardened. His anger and his resentment would disappear with one fell stroke. He would enjoy her matchless body one last time. He would take his pleasure and pleasure her in return.

And she would spend the rest of her life remembering it.

'Some of the major shareholders from the drug company I'm trying to buy are in town,' he said evenly. 'They've financed an art-house film which looks as if it's going to be a commercial success.'

She blinked. 'You mean they invest in films *and* drug companies?'

He walked over to the mirror which hung over an ornate marble fireplace and adjusted his tie. 'Why not? They like to spread their investments around. It's how you make the big bucks.'

'And where do I fit in?'

He turned back to face her, his expression unreadable. 'You'll accompany me to the screening and afterwards we're having dinner with the stars of the film, who are over here promoting it. All you have to do is gaze at me adoringly, *tesoro*. You play the young wife eager to get back with her husband. Do you think you can manage that?'

His words were wry but Nicole wondered what he would do if he knew the truth. That behind her nonchalant air, her senses were on fire. That every time he even looked at her she wanted to melt. She dug her fingernails into the sequins on her handbag. And he *mustn't* find out because then he might start touching her again. And she *wanted* him to do it to her again—that was the most dangerous thing of all. Next time she might not be strong enough to resist him.

'Oh, I think I can just about manage to maintain the façade of adoring you for a few hours—just so long as we're back before midnight strikes,' she said coolly. 'Just give me a couple of minutes and I'll go and fetch my wrap.'

But that sense of unreality she'd felt earlier swept over her again as she climbed into the back of Rocco's car—this time with the brooding billionaire by her side. She tried to make conversation but sensed that Rocco could see right through her attempts at chit-chat. Was he aware that it was all she could do not to reach out her hand and caress the honed hardness of his taut thigh, or run her fingertips through the ebony ruffle of his hair? Could he guess she was fantasising about him pressing the button which would bring down the screen shielding them from the driver, before lying her on the back seat and pulling her panties down. Little beads of sweat spring out on her forehead as she started imagining his tongue exploring her heated flesh and Nicole was relieved when finally they reached the venue.

The place where the screening was fancier than anywhere he'd ever taken her and she was amazed he could seem so relaxed in such a high-profile setting, for the Rocco of old would have curled his sensual mouth with derision. Flashbulbs popped as they walked up the flower-decked red carpet, his guiding hand placed unnervingly in the small of her back and making her shiver, despite the warmth of the evening.

The lights went down and the big screen lit up and Nicole watched a film which didn't really do it for her, even though everyone else seemed to love it. She'd never been a big fan of black and white movies and, besides, she was distracted by what was going on in the semi-darkness. She noticed that the American actress who was starring in the picture and seated on Rocco's other side was spending an awful lot of time cupping her hand over his ear to whisper into it. And suddenly all Nicole's defiant words about nobody being able to tell the difference between real and fake jewellery seemed like so much hot air, because Anna Rivers looked a class act in her waterfall of diamonds, with the burly man from security who was guarding them never far from her side. Nicole shot her a glance, aware that the beautiful actress was flirting outrageously with her husband and that she didn't like it. She didn't like it one bit.

Afterwards, they ate dinner in the Café de Monaco,

an award-winning restaurant which overlooked the harbour. Yet despite not having eaten anywhere this grand for a long time, the experience was wasted on Nicole. She seemed to have lost her appetite and the glass of champagne she'd drunk at the beginning of the evening had left her with nothing but a raging thirst. But she was determined to honour her side of this crazy bargain and did her best to chat as agreeably as she could to the various shareholders. She treated them as if they were prospective customers in her little Cornish pottery shop and tried not to be offended by their obvious surprise when they learned who she was. Even the star of the film gaped like a stranded fish when she overheard Nicole talking.

'You are Rocco's *wife*?' clarified Anna Rivers slowly.

'I am,' agreed Nicole.

The actress frowned. 'But I didn't even know he was married.'

'Well, there you go,' said Nicole weakly, feeling a total fraud—although she was unable to deny her satisfaction when the actress spent the rest of the evening talking to her leading man instead of trying to monopolise Rocco.

Nicole stood there in her plain black dress, flashing a friendly smile whenever anyone looked in her direction. At one point she was targeted by an Argentinian ex-polo player, Javier Estrada—a flirtatious man with flashing black eyes who frankly left her cold. As the evening drew to a close, she found herself in animated conversation with Annelise, the wife of Marcel Dupois—the conservative shareholder Rocco had warned her about.

The Frenchwoman turned out to have a passion for pottery so they had lots to talk about and when Nicole lifted her head it was to meet Rocco's questioning gaze burning into her like bright blue fire.

Gaze back at him adoringly, she told herself. Act like a wife who wants to make up with arguably the best-looking man in the room. She managed a passable imitation of adulation and her cheeks flared in response to the answering intensity in his eyes. He didn't look away and neither did she and for a few extraordinary seconds the make-believe felt almost real. Her chest tightened and suddenly she was having difficulty breathing. How was it possible to want a man yet hate him at the same time? To wish he were close, yet want to push him as far away as possible? Quickly, she turned away and stared out at the lights which were glittering in the harbour, trying to drink in a view which would soon be nothing more than a fast-fading memory.

'Nicole?'

The sound of Rocco's voice made her tremble and silently Nicole cursed it. She found herself remembering the way he'd purred her name like that when he had been unzipping her jeans on the terrace—and wasn't she now in danger of playing out the memory in a little too much detail? Composing her face into a smile, she turned round, trying very hard not to react to the wicked gleam in his eyes.

'Rocco!' she said brightly. 'Hi.'

His eyes mocked her. 'Hi.'

'Are you—' she swallowed '—having a good time?'

He shrugged. 'Tolerable. But I think we've had

enough partying for one night, don't you? We should think about going.'

It was an unequivocal statement intended to terminate the evening and Nicole wanted to protest. To say she was enjoying herself and could they please stay. But that was only delaying the inevitable—and why was she suddenly feeling so *nervous*? Just because she wanted him didn't mean anything was going to happen, did it? Women wanted men all the time but they didn't act on those desires. She certainly wasn't going to jeopardise everything she'd worked for by falling into the arms of a man who spelled nothing but danger.

Her smile didn't slip as she tucked her clutch bag under her arm. 'Sure. Why not?'

In the limousine Rocco was silent, staring out at the principality's glitzy shops as they drove by, as if he'd never really noticed them before. And Nicole did the same—concentrating on the steep roads and the breathtaking views of the harbour as the powerful car gained height. She told herself she was glad he didn't want to engage in meaningless chatter but in truth the silence was unsettling her. At least talking would have been a distraction from the growing awareness inside her body—the unwanted tingling of her breasts and the heat pooling low in her belly, which was making her feel like a victim of her own desire. It was all she could do not to squirm impatiently on the seat beside him and beg him to put her out of her misery with the hard pressure of his kiss.

'You did very well tonight,' he said when at last the car drew up outside his house. 'I could see how well you connected with Annelise Dupois. She obviously thought you were very engaging.'

'Thanks.'

'Our Argentinian friend certainly thought so, too,' he added drily. 'You seem to have won yourself a new fan.'

'As did you,' she said sweetly. 'Why, Anna Rivers could barely contain her dismay when she discovered I was your wife.'

In the semi-darkness his eyes gleamed like a jungle predator who had suddenly appeared from behind thick foliage. 'So we have discovered that we are both attractive to the opposite sex,' he observed.

'Hardly ground-breaking news where you're concerned, Rocco.'

'And that we can both be somewhat…*territorial* about each other.'

The lightness in her voice didn't quite come off. 'Speak for yourself.'

'Oh, I am. But you can hardly deny your own irritation whenever Anna whispered in my ear,' he said wryly. 'Since it was written all over your face.'

Had she been that transparent? 'I noticed you didn't try to stop her. Were you enjoying her warm breath on your earlobe and the way she was giggling hysterically at practically everything you said?'

He shrugged. 'Not really. I was more interested in your reaction.'

'I was acting, Rocco—that was all. Trying to play the part of the reconciling wife who would have been jealous at such an interaction. You really shouldn't read anything more into it than that.'

She reached for the door handle and the waiting chauffeur must have been watching because immediately he jumped out to open the door and Nicole stepped from the claustrophobic atmosphere of the car. As she felt the warm Mediterranean air wash over her skin, she knew she needed to get a grip. To ask herself why she was feeling so possessive about a man who only ever tolerated her. And then to stop it.

Veronique must have been off duty because Rocco unlocked the door himself and the absence of servants made their homecoming seem curiously normal. Only it wasn't normal, Nicole reminded herself fiercely. That was just another figment of her overactive imagination.

'I'm tired,' she said. 'I'm going to bed. Goodnight, Rocco.'

'Goodnight, Nicole.' He didn't try to stop her.

Had she thought he might?

Of course she had. Her body was in such a heightened state of desire that she felt almost deflated when she pushed open the door to the bedroom suite she had chosen—as far away from Rocco as possible—and clicked it shut behind her.

Stripping off the black jersey dress and letting the worthless gems spool into a green heap on one of the modern glass tables, Nicole gathered her hair up beneath a voluminous plastic cap and went to stand beneath the gushing shower. But rubbing soap over breasts which were already aroused and imagining it was Rocco's dark fingers sliding between her thighs instead of her own was not the relaxing experience she'd been anticipating. In fact, when she turned off the jets of water, she felt even more churned up than she had done in the limousine.

She dried her skin and raked a wide-toothed comb through her curls but she was feeling much too edgy to think about sleeping. The moon was so bright that it was flooding the room with silver light and, pulling on a baggy T-shirt and slipping on a clean pair of panties, she walked across the room towards the terrace and stepped outside, the tiles cool beneath her bare feet. Above her the dark sky was punctured by the bright glitter of stars and the moon was huge as she leaned her elbows against the wrought-iron railings and stared out at the inky gleam of the sea.

Had she been crazy to come here?

Probably.

She realised it was going to be hard to forget Rocco after this and it had nothing to do with the fancy house, or cars, or the yacht he'd casually mentioned was moored in the harbour. It was being in his company again. She'd forgotten how charismatic he was and what a powerful magnetism he exerted over everyone, but especially over her. She'd forgotten because it had been in her best interests to forget and she had been trying to move on. But now she was confused and aching. He hadn't kissed her tonight—he hadn't even *touched* her—and yet it was as if he'd started a slow blaze inside her. A drift of wind lifted the curls from the back of her neck and she sighed, realising that sleep wasn't going to come easily. Still, nobody ever died from a lack of sleep, did they? She would just stand there and watch the moonlight glinting on the water and wait until her eyelids started growing heavy.

She heard the click of the bedroom door as it opened but she didn't turn round. She didn't need to. Nobody else would walk into her bedroom uninvited. Nobody else would dare. But even if a hundred people had pushed open that door, she would have known it was Rocco from a hundred paces. Was she so sensitive to his presence that she could detect him—like some animal who had sniffed out her natural mate in the wild? Was that why her nipples had started puckering so that she wanted to open her mouth to cry out that they were craving his touch?

He was moving across the room and the only other sound she could hear was the amplified pounding of her heart above his approaching footsteps.

Tell him to go, she thought.

Beg him to stay.

'Nicole?'

Like rich velvet, his voice filtered through the warm air and Nicole shivered as he stepped out onto the terrace behind her. Had she thought the spoken word would shatter the spell he'd managed to weave without even being in her eyeline? Because if so, she had completely misread the situation.

'What?' she said, in what was surely the most pointless question of all time.

'Turn around,' he said.

She told herself she was going to resist—but how could she? She felt herself turning in response to his sultry command and suddenly realised it wasn't resentment she felt, but *relief.* Yes, relief. Because wasn't this shimmering feeling of excitement better than the half-dead way she'd felt at the end of their marriage? Wasn't it good to feel properly *alive* again in a way she hadn't felt for a long time? 'What do you want, Rocco?'

'You know damned well what I want.' His lips twisted into a predatory smile. 'I want you.'

And, oh, the feeling was mutual. She wanted him to take away this terrible aching and the deep well of loneliness inside her but it was a risk—and a big one. What if having sex only increased her desire for him instead of killing it? Restlessly she shifted beneath his shadowed gaze, knowing it was a risk she was prepared to take because the thought of sending him away was intolerable. One more night, that was all. One night to finally rid herself of these lingering demons. All she needed to remember was to be on her guard against un-wanted emotion because it had no place in what was about to happen. Rocco was programmed to want sex and she was programmed to want something deeper—because that was what women did. And love was some-thing she would never get from Rocco Barberi.

So she stood beneath the silver spotlight of the moon and wondered if her expression gave away the hun-ger which was snaring her with its silken tendrils. He was wearing nothing but jeans—the top button undone so that dark hair arrowed down towards the ridge-like bulge pushing against his crotch. His chest was glow-ing and an arrogant smile was curving his lips as if he was already anticipating her surrender. And Nicole knew then that if she did this, it was going to have to be on her own terms.

She needed to remember they were equals. He wasn't her boss and soon he wouldn't even be her husband. This was physical, that was all. It was what grown-ups did. They had carefully considered sex which they could walk away from with nothing but a glow of satisfaction. She tried to iron out the emotion from her voice but she could hear an underlying tremble as she answered him. 'So what are we going to do about it?'

'I think you know the answer to that.' In the moonlight his eyes glittered. 'Get undressed,' he said softly.

CHAPTER SIX

THE CONTROL IN Rocco's voice threatened to destroy the sensual mood which had ensnared her and Nicole stared at him resentfully. Did he think she was the same grateful virgin he'd first seduced, who would do whatever it was he demanded?

She held his gaze, her chin tilting as he studied her with cool calculation. 'What did you say?'

He gave a soft laugh. 'You heard.'

'I want you to repeat it, Rocco.'

There was a pause. 'I told you to get undressed.'

'To perform a striptease for you, you mean?'

He shrugged. 'If you like.'

'Well, I don't like,' she said. 'Not any more. I've changed, Rocco—haven't you?'

His eyes gleamed but he didn't answer her question directly. 'So why don't you tell me what you *do* like?'

And despite everything she knew and everything she had learnt, Nicole found herself wishing for the impossible. Wanting him to say something romantic. To tell her he'd missed her and his life hadn't been the same since she'd gone. Wouldn't a few tender words enhance what was about to happen, even if he didn't mean them? So that for a while she could pretend he cared, as she'd pretended so often in the past. But that would be a pointless thing to do because grown-ups didn't demand hypocritical words. They accepted things exactly the way they were. And this was sex—farewell sex or break-up sex, whatever you wanted to call it. One last taste of Rocco Barberi's magnificent body—and hadn't she better make the most of it?

Raking her fingers back through her still-damp curls, she was aware that her hardened nipples were thrusting against her T-shirt and his eyes were following the movement, like a man hypnotised. Briefly she revelled in a feeling of power as she met the smoky hunger of his gaze. 'I want you to take off my clothes for me,' she said huskily. 'And to do it as slowly as possible. I want you to test your own patience—so we're both so turned on that we can't bear it a second longer. That's what I'd *like*, Rocco.'

His eyes narrowed, suspicion shadowing them. 'Since when did you start having fantasies like that?' he demanded, in a low voice. '*Has* there been another man?'

'You think I don't have any kind of imagination? Or that I'm incapable of articulating my own desires unless a man shows me how? Oh, wow.' She shook her head. 'Thanks for reminding me how unspeakably arrogant you can be, Rocco—and for making me realise that this would be a very bad idea.'

She went to walk past him, her hair swaying in the breeze from the terrace, but he caught hold of her and pulled her up hard against him. She could feel her breasts flattening against his bare chest through her T-shirt and hear the wild patter of her heart.

'I don't think you want to go anywhere, do you, Nicole? Not really. You just want to play provocative and you want me to do the same.' His finger traced down the side of her face, before coming to rest against the throbbing pulse at her neck. 'Have I got that right?'

She attempted a shrug which didn't quite come off because showing bravado was one thing—but not quite so easy when his face was just inches away and all his hard, honed flesh was this close. 'I'm not slipping into old patterns,' she said huskily. 'I'm not stripping for you just because you've snapped your fingers. I don't want to play those games any more. If you want me naked, then you'll have to undress me yourself.'

A smile touched his lips. 'Is that so?'

She nodded, unable to speak because now his hand was drifting from her face down her body and she wished her T-shirt weren't so baggy. What had possessed her to wear such an unflattering garment? As if he'd read her thoughts, he rucked up the material to slip his hand underneath so that his fingertips were on her bare skin and her nerve-endings were instantly fired as she felt that first light touch.

'So how slow would you like me to go?' he questioned almost conversationally as he cupped one of her breasts luxuriously in the palm of his hand and began to massage the underside of it with the edge of his thumb. 'How long shall I take before I remove this delightful piece of clothing you're wearing?'

Nicole's knees sagged. 'Oh,' she said breathlessly.

'You're not making yourself very clear, Nicole. Oh, what?'

'I don't…' She closed her eyes. 'I don't remember.'

'Sudden memory lapse, *tesoro*?' he murmured, his Sicilian accent a velvety caress. 'I wonder what might be causing it?'

Nicole couldn't answer because now his thumb was flicking across her thrusting nipple, sending little ripples of pleasure criss-crossing over her skin. He stroked tiny circles over the engorged flesh before turning his attention to the other breast and Nicole could feel her frustration begin to mount. Squirming beneath his touch, she wondered why on earth she'd told him she wanted this done slowly when already her desire was so intense that she could feel a honeyed heat between her thighs. She wanted—no, *needed*—to get horizontal but he showed no sign of moving and she realised that, in order to stop her knees from buckling, she was going to have to cling onto his shoulders to anchor herself. He gave a soft laugh as her fingers dug into his flesh and he buried his mouth in her neck, his lips becoming entangled with the wild spill of curls as he drifted the tip of his tongue over her skin.

'R-Rocco,' she whispered.

'What?'

'Take…take off my T-shirt.'

'I thought you told me to take my time. To stretch my own patience were the words I think you used. And believe me, *tesoro*—I haven't even started yet. I'll show you just how patient I can be.'

It was both a promise and a threat—as well as a boastful demonstration of just how controlled he could be—and Nicole closed her eyes as he ran the flat of his hand over her belly, taking care to avoid the place where she most wanted to be touched. She bit her lip. Had she really been so sure of herself to think she could wait when she so desperately wanted to feel him inside her? She squirmed as deliberately he inched his way along the lacy edge of her panties, praying for him to slip his finger inside so that he could feel how much she wanted him, but he didn't. She had wanted to control what was happening by setting the pace, but she had done the exact opposite and given him all the power. She wondered what the hell she'd been playing at.

So what was she waiting for?

She was his equal—remember?

Reaching between them, she tugged down the zipper of his jeans, feeling his hard length spring against her palm as she freed him, and his words were a muffled moan as she began to stroke him.

'I thought you said—'

'I changed my mind,' she whispered. 'It's a woman's prerogative, Rocco—hadn't you heard?'

With her thumb and her forefinger she began to tease his taut erection but he halted her fingers with the firm clamp of his own and she heard him give an unsteady laugh.

She stared at him indignantly. 'What's so funny?'

'You are. I had no idea you could be so…mercurial. I like it.'

A prick of sadness threatened to puncture Nicole's

blissful state. Of course he hadn't known what she was capable of and had never bothered finding out *because he hadn't really cared*. To Rocco she would always be the office cleaner in the too small uniform with the mop and bucket in her hand—the last woman in the world he should have married.

But she wasn't going to think about that.

Not now.

She was going to think how good this felt and to enjoy every single second of it.

And then she was going to kiss him goodbye.

'I'm pleased you like it but you'd better not get used to it,' she warned softly.

'To what?'

'The sex.'

He raised his eyebrows. 'Oh?'

'Since we both know this is only going to happen once.'

'Is that so?' He seemed to recover himself then and Nicole saw the light of challenge in his eyes as he peeled off her T-shirt with a fluid movement and carried her over to the bed. 'In that case maybe we should stop wasting so much time talking and get down to business.'

'You're obsessed with business,' she said faintly as he put her down on the bed, and he laughed. Nicole watched him fishing around in the pocket of his jeans before kicking them off and joining her. And suddenly he was towering over her, one knee pressed on either side of her hips as she lay there naked, except for her brief pair of lacy black panties.

'So how do you want it?' he murmured. 'Fast? Slow? Lights on? Off?'

She wanted to tell him not to be so flippant until she realised that too would be wasting time. He was right. What was the point of talking when she wanted him so badly that her heart was threatening to burst right out of her chest? Why bother trying to score points when none of this meant anything? She looked up into the unfathomable gleam of his eyes and spoke from the heart. 'Make love to me,' she said.

She saw his features tense as he stroked her hair away from her face and for a moment she thought he was going to kiss her. But he didn't. Instead, he began to explore her—his fingers drifting erotic pathways over her body as he reacquainted himself with skin which wouldn't seem to stop shivering. He hooked his fingers into the sides of her panties and she thought he might rip them off as he'd done so many times before but he didn't—though she noticed his hand was unsteady as he slid them down over her knees. Greedily, her lips pressed against the silken flesh of his shoulder as she parted her thighs for him.

'Mmm… So responsive,' he breathed as she arched up towards him. 'That much never changes, does it, Nicole?'

But Nicole didn't want comparisons. She didn't want a then-and-now scenario, which might alert all those little indicators of pain which she'd blocked but which were just waiting to spring out if she wasn't careful. And this was supposed to be about pleasure, not pain. So take what you want and give him something in return. Wipe the slate clean so you can walk away from each other and leave the past where it belongs.

Exploring each of his nipples with a feather-light touch, she enjoyed the muffled groan he gave in response, watching his eyes flutter to a close as she drifted her fingertips down over the taut dip of his belly. She smoothed the symmetrical ridges of his ribs and thought, not for the first time, how magnificent his naked body was, the olive skin glowing invitingly against the whiteness of the sheet. This was a feast for all the senses, she thought. She could taste him and feel him and she could smell him, too—that beguiling scent of bergamot underpinned with a raw masculinity, which she breathed in with each unsteady intake of air.

Did he hear how erratic her breathing had become? Was that what prompted him to push her back against the pillows so he could bend his head to her breasts, his tongue cleaving a moist path over each tender mound until they were so acutely aroused that she began to writhe impatiently? His teeth grazed over her hardened nipples as his hand moved between her thighs—and Nicole gave a yelp of pleasure as he moved his finger against her moist slickness. And, oh, she had missed this—she was only just realising how much. She could feel the inexorable build of heat and remembered the way she'd almost come apart in his arms when they'd been outside on the terrace earlier that day and, dazedly, she opened her eyes. 'No,' she whispered.

'No?' he echoed incredulously, his accent growing deeper as it always did during moments of intense pleasure. 'You choose this moment to change your mind?'

'I meant not…not like that,' she amended breathlessly.

He understood immediately and in the moonlight she saw hunger darkening his rugged features as he reached for the condom he had taken from his jeans. She watched while he ripped the foil open and stroked the rubber over his aroused length and the intimacy of the simple action was almost her undoing. Because hadn't he taught her how to do that and to turn it into a kind of erotic foreplay, a task she had happily undertaken? And hadn't he turned on her that time and asked her if she'd punctured the condom with her fingernails—demanded to know if she'd deliberately tried to get herself pregnant? He'd retracted the accusation immediately but the memory had lingered for a long time afterwards.

Yet all those dark thoughts vanished the moment he entered her and were replaced by a feeling of such completion that it took Nicole's breath away. How easily pleasure could conquer pain, she thought. Could make you so helpless that you barely knew who you were any more. Suddenly you forgot you were a wife who was seeking a divorce and became that same blown-away creature who had given her innocence to him so willingly.

'Rocco,' she said, brokenly.

He didn't answer. He was too busy doing all the things he knew she loved best. Hooking her quivering thighs around his hips to angle himself just right. Cupping her buttocks and bringing them towards him—the slick action making his penetration all the deeper. And despite knowing that for him this was nothing more than physical, Nicole was lost. Lost in sensation as one thrust followed another and the sweet and familiar layers began to build. She wanted it to last all night but that was never going to happen—not when she was in such a heightened state of arousal. She'd almost dissolved from the moment he entered her and now she couldn't hold it back any longer.

'I'm coming,' she whispered.

'I know you are, *tesoro*,' he whispered back, his voice deep and husky.

The murmured intimacy of that comment broke through the last of her resistance and Nicole felt herself dissolve around him. Through shuddered little gasps she could feel her legs splaying and her back arching. He gave a low growl of appreciation as she began to convulse around him and rogue tears pricked at her eyes as Rocco's own movements became more urgent. She knew from the tension in his body just how close he was to the edge and she gripped his shoulders as he drove into her like a man possessed. And didn't she revel in the fact that she could still do this to him? Could still make him moan like that as his body jerked with his own powerful orgasm?

There was silence in the room afterwards as his dark head lay pressed against her neck. Staring over his shoulder at the moon-dappled ceiling, Nicole wanted to say something reassuring. To make some cool and clever remark which would make him realise this meant nothing to her. Something to reassure him that she wasn't reading too much into what had been just sex. But instead she found herself whispering the only thing which was on her mind. 'Rocco.'

Rocco grew still as he heard her murmur his name like that, trying to regain the control he'd lost from the moment he'd entered her voluptuous body. The way she touched him unsettled him and the way she said his name unsettled him even more because she sounded confused. And wasn't the truth that he was feeling pretty confused himself? Tangling his fingers in the curls which flowed down her back, he told himself this was all he had wanted. Having her underneath him and hearing her gasp out his name one last time had been the whole point of the exercise. He'd wanted her and now he'd had her—which meant he could just walk away. Could give her the divorce she so desperately wanted and set them both free.

But suddenly it didn't seem that simple and walking away no longer looked such an attractive prospect. Instead he found his hand straying to her breast and his fingers teasing a pouting nipple into life all over again as he waited for her little murmur of assent. For the silent wriggle of her curvy hips to indicate that she'd acknowledged his hardness growing inside her and wanted it to happen all over again. Only this time she wasn't so accommodating and instead of wrapping her luscious thighs around his back, she was pulling out from under him and wriggling away, until she was lying on the far side of the mattress—so far away that she might have been on a different planet. He turned his head to see the set of her profile as she stared up at the ceiling, where the moon shadows were dancing in an undulating display of light and shade.

'Is that it?' he questioned.

The slight nod of her head was the only indication she'd heard him and when she spoke it was in a voice he didn't recognise. 'What were you anticipating, Rocco? Another bout of wild sex? Round number two?'

'Why not?' His gaze settled on her hardened nipples, dark against the silver wash of her breasts, and he thought how her body was contradicting the conviction of her feisty words. 'The first time is simply the appetiser—the second time is the feast. Surely you remember that, Nicole?'

He watched her throat constrict as she swallowed and he could hear the stiffness in her voice as she answered.

'The circumstances are rather different this time around.'

'In what way?' he drawled.

She shrugged. 'We obviously both enjoyed that—in a physical sense, certainly. Perhaps it's better not to tempt fate by doing it again.'

'And if I don't agree?'

'I'm afraid you don't have any choice but to agree, Rocco.'

There was a pause and when he spoke his voice was very calm. It was the same kind of thoughtful response he might have used if someone had raised an awkward question in a board meeting. 'I thought you wanted me to be accommodating about the forthcoming divorce.'

Slowly, she turned her head to meet his eyes and he thought how beautiful she looked with her dark curls all wild and free and the faint flush which had spread from her cheeks to her breasts.

'Is that a threat?' she demanded. 'Are you saying

that if I don't agree to have sex with you again, you'll block the petition?'

'Please, Nicole. Do not insult me. I would not dream of asking you to do anything you don't want to do.' He reached across the bed to place his palm over her thigh, pleased but unsurprised by the instinctive quiver of her flesh in response. 'I'm merely pointing out that it seems a waste for us not to capitalise on our remarkable chemistry while we have the opportunity to do so.'

She pushed his hand away even though he could sense her reluctance.

'You mean the chemistry which got us into so much trouble in the first place?'

'Is that how you see it?'

'Of course it is. Because it's the truth, Rocco, and one I made myself accept a long time ago. I was just another body. Just another face. Just another one of the long list of women you seduced. The only difference between me and the others was that I was a virgin.' She reached for the rumpled duvet which lay at the foot of the bed before yanking it up, though he noticed she didn't include him in the protective cover she gathered round herself. With only her face visible, she stared at him and her bottom lip was jutting out stubbornly. 'And you felt differently about that. Perhaps you were jaded because you'd had so many experienced women throwing themselves at you. Wasn't that the way of it, Rocco?'

His answering smile was hard. 'That first night with you blew my mind.'

'The thrill of breaking through my hymen, I suppose? That unique tightness which you can never get back.'

He stiffened, unfamiliar with the sudden steel which had entered her voice. 'You have become very cynical, Nicole.'

Shivering violently despite the warm cloud of duvet which enveloped her, Nicole wanted to ask what on earth he expected. Had he thought she'd just walked away from him without having learned anything? Because if you didn't learn from your mistakes then what hope was there? She'd realised that in order to survive she needed to view what had happened dispassionately, and there was nothing to be gained from trying to put a sentimental slant on her failed marriage. The giddy virgin who'd fallen for the powerful Sicilian was now just a distant memory and she'd worked hard on gaining a whole load of perspective in the interim. She didn't fabricate myths or believe impossible things any more, just to make herself feel better. And a single bout of fantastic sex with the man she had married was not going to make her change her opinion.

She realised there was something else they hadn't talked about—something far bigger than a young women being introduced to sex for the first time—but she couldn't face bringing up the subject of their baby. Her fingers tightened around the duvet. Not tonight. Maybe not ever. He hadn't wanted to talk about it at the time, had he?

And neither had she, she realised, with a sudden flash of insight. *Rocco's reluctance to communicate had suited her very well. He hadn't wanted to talk about what had happened to them, while she had simply been unable to articulate her pain. Had that made the void even deeper?*

She sucked in a deep breath, resolutely bringing her thoughts back to the present. 'Maybe I needed a touch of cynicism. Maybe I was too much of an innocent in all senses of the word,' she said, aware of the sudden prick of tears at the backs of her eyes and terrified he might see them. 'And now I think it's time you went back to your own bed.'

He shifted his weight slightly on the mattress. 'Or I could stay here and spend the night making love to you. Since that is what we both want.'

And despite everything which was wrong between them, Nicole was tempted. Who wouldn't be tempted by such a man? He looked like a lion lying there, so certain of his own strength as the moon coated his powerful body with silver. A quick glance told her that the faint arousal she'd felt while he was still inside her was now fully grown, and didn't the irrational side of her na-ture—the hungry, yearning side—make her long to put her arms around him and have him do it all over again?

But that way lay a madness which would blur her shaky hold on reality. Already she felt weakened by the realisation of how deeply he could still affect her. She wondered what had happened to the woman who was supposed to be over him—but deep down she knew the answer. That woman didn't—maybe couldn't—exist when Rocco held her in his arms. Why make herself vulnerable to him by having more sex when she still had the rest of the weekend to get through?

'I think I'll pass on that,' she said, the surprise on his rugged features only increasing her resolve. She gave him a thin smile. 'And now I want to go to sleep. Alone.'

He made no attempt to persuade her, rising from the bed in a display of muscular grace—his buttocks pale against the dark olive of his powerful thighs. But as he bent to pick up his jeans Nicole turned onto her stomach and buried her face in the soft pillow, trying to block out the rasping sound of his zip. She heard the door click quietly shut behind him but her emotions were too jangled to even think of sleep.

And she realised that not once during that entire episode had he kissed her.

CHAPTER SEVEN

'WHAT CAN I bring you for *le petit dejeuner, madame*?'

Her eyelids feeling as heavy as lead, Nicole sat down at the table which had been laid up for breakfast on the terrace, momentarily dazzled by the crystal and silver which gleamed in the early morning sunshine. The air was warm with the combined scent of jasmine and strong coffee and Veronique was gazing at her expectantly.

'We have bread and croissants, *madame*,' the housekeeper continued. 'Though Signor Barberi has reminded chef that it is the English way to eat a cooked breakfast—should you wish for bacon and eggs.'

Nicole smiled, even though smiling was the last thing she felt like doing. Pulling a face full of remorse would surely be more appropriate in the circumstances. After a restless night haunted by disturbing dreams she had woken up amid sex-scented sheets, revelling in the delicious glow of her body until the heart-sinking moment when she'd remembered exactly what had made it feel that way. Or rather, who.

An image of her unzipping Rocco's jeans and caress-

ing him intimately rushed into her head and her cheeks
burned as, hastily, she put on a pair of sunglasses and
pulled her coffee towards her, wishing that last night
wouldn't keep flooding back in a conflicting rush of
hungry and humiliating memories. Her cheeks burned
as she recalled the way she had welcomed her husband
into her body with an urgency which had taken her by
surprise—startled her in the discovery that her desire
for him was stronger than ever. And that had puzzled
her. Because at the tail end of their marriage, hadn't she
resigned herself to the fact that she no longer wanted
Rocco anywhere near her?

And he hadn't wanted her either, had he? They had
pushed each other away in every sense of the word.
She watched the breeze tugging at the pink petals of
the roses at the centrepiece of the table and tucked her
hair behind her ears. Last night shouldn't have happened
but there was nothing she could do about it now. She
couldn't wind back the clock and wish she'd suggested
Rocco take a hike when he'd wandered into her bedroom—*uninvited*—and told her to undress.

But her sexual gymnastics had left her with a raven-
ous appetite and hungrily Nicole eyed the dish of iced
peaches before looking up at the housekeeper. 'I'd love
some poached eggs,' she said. 'With wholemeal toast,
if that's possible.'

'*D'accord, madame.*'

After Veronique had gone, Nicole ate some fruit and
watched the expensive yachts bobbing in the exclusive
harbour until the housekeeper returned with the rest
of her breakfast. She was busy dipping a rectangle of

toast into the runny yolk of an egg and oblivious to the presence of anything else when a shadow fell over the table and she looked up to see Rocco standing there, obviously fresh from the shower. His black hair was curling in shiny tendrils around his neck and his jaw looked newly shaved. Unjacketed, his ice-blue shirt contrasted with the much darker hue of his eyes and those exquisitely cut trousers emphasised his long legs. Her breakfast forgotten, Nicole stared up at him and all that blatant masculinity so early in the morning began to do worrying things to her pulse-rate.

'Rocco!' she accused. 'Do you always make a habit of creeping up on people like that?'

'I move quietly, *tesoro*. It is in my nature. It's only because you're so damned jumpy that you react like that,' he drawled, drawing out a chair opposite her and lowering himself onto it.

Nicole put her toast back on the plate because eating had suddenly lost its allure. Those thighs, she thought with unwilling hunger, unable to forget their tensile power as he'd driven into her last night. She grabbed her napkin and blotted it over her lips. 'Maybe it's just you who has that effect on me.'

He leaned across the table to pour himself a cup of coffee. 'Should I be flattered?'

She met his gaze. 'What do you think?'

He shrugged. 'I never know what to think where you're concerned, Nicole. Take last night, for example. One minute you're hot for me and the next as cold as ice. You are something of an…enigma.'

She gave a short laugh. 'That's rich, coming from you. The man who never talks about his feelings.'

'Because that is not my way,' he said, lifting the cup to his lips and sipping from it. 'You know that. It has never been the way of Barberi men.'

Nicole pushed her plate away. That much was true. She thought about his grandfather, the man who had helped bring up Rocco and his siblings after their parents had been killed in the dramatic speedboat accident which had been splashed across the front pages of the world's press. She remembered the day she had arrived at the family complex just outside Palermo, fresh from her honeymoon and slightly daunted at meeting the patriarch of Sicily's most powerful clan for only the second time since her wedding. Very quickly she'd discovered that the revered elder was as uptight as Rocco about expressing his feelings. She'd thought his lack of warmth was because Turi was an old-fashioned man who would have preferred his golden-boy heir to have married a Sicilian woman with an equally elevated status.

Yet despite the barriers she'd encountered, Nicole had been determined to overcome them and make a good impression. She'd wanted to fit in, no matter what it took, because she'd wanted to make a proper family home for her new husband and their baby. She had spent most of her American honeymoon—when she wasn't being sick—trying to learn as much Italian as possible in order to impress her new family and especially Rocco's grandfather. But everything had seemed so new and strange and different when she'd arrived in Sicily. She had felt like a lonely outsider in the huge and sprawling house with nothing much to do all day and nobody to talk to. Rocco had buried himself in work and Turi had spoken only in dialect so that they had barely been able to communicate with each other. Like grandfather, like grandson, she remembered thinking. Maybe her mistake had been to expect anything different. To think that the orphaned nobody who had mopped floors could ever have been considered *suitable*.

And it was weird. Rocco spoke of *her* inability to discuss her feelings as if it were a character flaw, while for him it was simply something he accepted as a natural trait of Barberi men. Meanwhile, he showed no inclination to change. He was still concealing his feelings—if he had any—behind the weapons of blame and possession. He was a hugely successful man with a massive global influence, who examined business opportunities in the most minute of detail. He was prepared to bring her out here in order to facilitate a deal, yet he was able to ignore the deep, dark hole at the centre of their marriage and make as if it had never happened.

He was acting as if they had never created a baby together. As if that brief little life had never existed.

Her heart contracted with pain and suddenly Nicole knew that she couldn't carry on not knowing. Maybe that was why this whole relationship felt so...*unfinished*. She recognised now that she must shoulder some of the blame, because she had run away rather than face up to their issues. But she was here now, wasn't she? Maybe it needed to be resolved once and for all before either of them could have true peace. Was it that which gave her the courage to come right out and say it? The sense that she would never get the answers she sought unless she pushed for them, no matter how painful that might be?

She removed her dark glasses and looked at him. 'Okay,' she said, sitting back in the chair. 'We've both accused the other of never discussing our true feelings—'

'I don't remember putting it exactly like that,' he said.

'You called me an enigma,' she pointed out. 'So why don't we agree to ask each other a question and then answer it truthfully? No excuses—and no getting out of it.'

'You're proposing some kind of party game?'

'Don't deliberately misunderstand me, Rocco. That's not what it's about.'

His flattened lips indicated a lack of enthusiasm which bordered on contempt. 'No? And the purpose of this interrogation is…what?'

It was a bad sign he even had to ask but Nicole wasn't going to back down now. She leaned across the table towards him. 'Couldn't you just do it, Rocco? Just this once. Just to humour me?'

'Very well.' He gave an impatient sigh. 'As long as you are prepared to ask first.'

How typical of him to say that! Nicole took a deep breath and started to speak and the words came rushing out before she had a chance to question the wisdom of saying them. 'You only married me because I was pregnant, didn't you?'

There was a pause. 'Yes,' he said at last.

She felt her heart twist as if someone were turning a corkscrew in her chest. She'd known that all along—so why did it hurt so much? Did hearing him say it mean

she could no longer pretend that her brief marriage had
been anything more than a sham?

She was tempted to abandon the conversation but
forced herself to continue. After all, they'd come this
far—which was further than they'd ever come before.
Why stop now? 'Now you,' she said, praying for him
to address the subject they'd both shied away from for
so long. She'd given him a lead by talking about her
pregnancy—all he had to do was take it from there
and confront the dark space which linked them both.
'Your turn.'

He took a sip of coffee before turning the full brilliance of his sapphire gaze on her. 'That's easy.' His
voice dipped into a seductive caress. 'Did you enjoy
last night?'

Nicole blinked and stared at him in dismay, unable to
believe he'd come out with something so…so…*super-
ficial*. Was that the only thing which mattered to him?
Sex? She swallowed. Maybe it was. Sex had been the
thing which had brought them together and remained
the only thing which united them.

'You mean, was I satisfied?' she demanded, her temper suddenly flaring. 'Yes, of course I was. You're very
good at satisfying a woman, Rocco—but you don't need
me to tell you that.'

It had been a mockery of a question and she suspected he'd asked it simply to even the score. To make
him an equal player in this 'game'—or maybe warn
her against ever trying to do something like this in future. But his attitude infuriated her. Couldn't he have
done the bigger thing and asked her about something

which mattered? No, of course he couldn't—because Rocco Barberi didn't *do* feelings. He acted like a machine and expected everyone else to do the same. And suddenly she knew she couldn't let this opportunity go. She was going to say it, no matter how much it angered him, or how much it brought back the pain. *Because she needed to say it.*

'You never talk about our child, Rocco.'

She saw a shadow briefly cloud his face but if she'd been expecting heartache, or anger, or pain, or longing, or any of the dark stream of emotions which had dragged her down into the depths of despair so many times, then she was about to be disappointed. Because Rocco was putting his cup down on the saucer as calmly as if she'd just asked him how often it rained in Monaco, his rugged features as impassive as she'd ever seen them, his blue eyes their habitual shade of cold.

'What is there to talk about?' he questioned tonelessly. 'It happened and there's nothing we can do to change it. We both wish it hadn't, but there you go.' He shrugged. 'I don't think there's anything more I can add to that and neither do I intend to.'

She wanted to shake him. To rail at him. To accuse him of being unfeeling and heartless—but how could she do that when he'd never pretended to be otherwise? Everything she'd ever wanted from Rocco Barberi, he was incapable of giving her. She had been determined to somehow win his love if only she tried hard enough. But love wasn't a competition you could win, she realised—and even if it was, surely having a winner would imply there had to be a loser.

And she didn't want to be that loser.

She didn't want to be anchored by the past. She wanted to be free of heartache and regret. Of him.

Briefly she thought about getting up from the table and telling Rocco she was going back to England and if he wanted to make her wait for her divorce, then she would just have to suck it up. But she had run away once before and where had that got her? It had left her with an underlying feeling of failure, no matter how many modest achievements she'd managed to chalk up along the way. Wasn't facing up to the truth like this—in a way they had never done in their marriage—a therapy of some kind, even if it hurt like hell?

But Rocco didn't hurt, did he? Rocco didn't give anything away. Not then and certainly not now.

Pushing back her chair, she rose to her feet and flung her napkin over her uneaten toast. 'Oh, what's the point of trying to talk to you?' she said. 'So why don't I make it easy for you, Rocco? Let's just spend the day apart and I'll join you for your cocktail party later. That way neither of us will have to endure a second more of each other's company than we need to. I'll be there for you in public and that's what matters. That was the deal, wasn't it?'

Rocco's eyes narrowed. He was aware that he had hurt her and wondered if that had been deliberate. Part of him had suspected that his blunt answers to her unwanted questions would have her running for the hills again—and wouldn't that have been simpler? Things were certainly less complicated when Nicole wasn't around, because she was turning into a constant stream of surprises. For a start, she wasn't intimidated by him. Not any more. She had the courage to ask him stuff and had been surprisingly calm when he'd given her the brutal truth.

At times during that uncomfortable conversation, she had clearly been trying to hold back her own feelings. There had been anger on her face and bitterness, too. And pain, of course—plenty of that. But no tears. He found himself wondering if it was a struggle for her to maintain that politely enquiring expression and from somewhere he felt the unfamiliar stab of his conscience. Had he been unnecessarily harsh with her?

'Yes, that was the deal,' he agreed slowly. 'But maybe we could amend it.'

'Really?' Their eyes locked. 'And just what did you have in mind, Rocco?'

It was unlike Rocco to search for the unspoken but he did so now. He saw the expression of resignation which had flattened her green eyes—as if sex was all he was capable of offering her. And even though up until a few minutes ago he might have echoed those very sentiments, now his ego rebelled against such an assumption. He would not tolerate being regarded as a stud, but it was more than that. Their conversation had left him feeling *disquieted*. He could see how vulnerable it had left his estranged wife, no matter how hard she tried to disguise it. And vulnerability was always a danger where women were concerned. It made them capable of misinterpreting an act of physical intimacy and loading it with imaginary significance. If they had sex right now, wouldn't it be asking for trouble?

He let his gaze drift over the simple white sundress which flattered her curvy body. She looked as sweet as on that first evening he'd met her, when she'd stood in front of him in her cleaner's uniform, looking guilty for having splashed him with soapy water. The fabric of his trousers had been warm and wet against his ankle but all he could remember was the emerald blaze of her eyes—and Rocco was unprepared for the sudden jolt of nostalgia he experienced.

His jaw clenched.

No. Sex would be a bad idea. He needed to get them as far away from the vicinity of a bedroom as possible and, for once, the idea of leaving her to sun herself by the pool while he buried himself in work was leaving him cold. 'Why don't I take you walking?' he said.

'Walking?' she echoed.

'I meant around the Rock.'

'The Rock?'

'That's what everyone calls Monaco. Because it's built on a rock,' he added.

'I'd kind of worked that one out for myself, Rocco.'

He gave a reluctant laugh as his gaze travelled to her feet—currently encased in a pair of high, strappy wedges which defined her shapely ankles and briefly made him regret his impetuous decision. 'Do you have anything more suitable you could wear?'

'Like trainers?'

'Trainers would be fine,' he said evenly. 'Why don't you go and put them on?'

Glad to escape the disturbing scrutiny of his gaze, Nicole sped upstairs, her heart pounding as she pushed open her bedroom door. She'd straightened the rumpled bedding before going down to breakfast but someone had obviously been in and changed the linen because now the bed looked so pristine that last night might never have happened. But it had. She could feel her cheeks heating as she located her sneakers, trying to forget their explosive passion and to remember instead what he'd just told her.

He had only married her because of the baby.

She remembered the doctor telling her that early miscarriage was very common. That she should go home to her husband and get pregnant again as soon as possible. But how could that be *possible* when Rocco had resolutely stayed away from her after she'd lost the baby? When he'd seemed almost *relieved* to have a legitimate reason not to resume marital relations. Was that how he'd felt only been afraid to admit it? Had some part of him recognised that the terrible thing which had happened was probably best in the long run, if it freed him from a marriage he had never intended?

But she had never asked him, had she? Had never sat him down or confronted him and not just because she was feeling out of her depth as the billionaire's new bride. She hadn't talked about stuff because, in a way, she hadn't known how. Those years in foster homes hadn't exactly been warm and although Peggy Watson had loved her like a mother, she had come from a fierce generation of practical Irishwomen who got on with things, rather than discussing how they made them *feel*.

Wasn't she as much to blame as Rocco for the lack of

communication between them at the time—which had speeded up the end of their forced marriage?

Tying her shoelaces, she grabbed a canvas tote bag and went back to the terrace to find him waiting, blue eyes gleaming as he quickly appraised her change of footwear.

'Much better,' he murmured.

Nicole's eyebrows shot up. 'Strange coming from the man who once insisted I parade about his office in a pair of sky-high stilettos. What happened, Rocco? Did your tastes undergo a dramatic change?'

His face was impassive. 'You are no longer my mistress, Nicole—that's what happened.'

But she'd felt like his mistress last night. He had treated her with that same raw hunger he'd displayed at the beginning of their relationship, before they were married. And that was something else which had always puzzled her, something else she had felt unable to ask him in the past. But now she had nothing left to lose and she looked unflinchingly into his bright eyes. 'Those things you used to get me to dress up in. The packages you used to buy from that shop in Soho—'

'You're going to tell me now that you didn't like them?' he questioned roughly.

'No,' she said slowly. 'I'm not going to say that. I wore them because you *did* like them. But the more outrageous the outfits, the more...*disapproving* you seemed to be, even though they clearly turned you on. It was as if you were trying to turn me into someone you could ultimately despise. Is that what you were doing, Rocco?'

Rocco felt his mouth dry. She was far more perceptive than he'd given her credit for, or maybe he'd just never stopped to notice it before. He'd been horrified to discover that the beautiful cleaner had been a virgin, because he hadn't wanted an innocent, he had wanted a *mistress*. Turning her onto the more colourful sexual practices enjoyed by his previous lovers had been an attempt to place her firmly into the latter category. Because the alternative was admitting he was captivated by having straightforward vanilla sex with his eager young lover. And that admission had made him uneasy because what then would she want from him—and could he ever be that man?

His mouth tightened. And then she'd fallen pregnant and once again he had been cast into the role which had haunted him all his life.

Responsible adult.

Ask Rocco.

See how Rocco does it.

Well, not any more.

He was free now and that was the way he liked it.

'Maybe I *was* trying to get you to despise me,' he admitted eventually.

Confusion fired in the leafy depths of her eyes. 'But why would you do that?'

He saw the colour which had risen to her cheeks and somehow he knew he couldn't duck out of this. 'Because I knew I was the type of man who could hurt you,' he said, in as candid an admission as he'd ever made. 'And I didn't want to do that. Not when I discovered just how sweet and innocent you really were.'

'Could you...elaborate, please?'

Rocco scowled, wondering why she was being so persistent when this was only going to hurt her. 'I thought that if I tried to objectify you, it would drive a wedge between us.'

'And it did,' she said dully.

'It did,' he agreed.

Her teeth were biting into the cushioned pinkness of her bottom lip but she said nothing more. She didn't have to. Her face gave it all away. That he'd ended up hurting her anyway. Because that was what he did. She'd tried to get close and he'd pushed her away. He didn't know any other way. *He didn't want it any other way.*

His gaze swept over her. 'So, have you changed your mind about sightseeing?'

She hesitated for a moment before shaking her head. 'Actually, I'm looking forward to it.'

He looked at her curiously. 'Despite the things I've just said?'

'Maybe *because* of the things you've just said,' she agreed then gave a shaky laugh. 'I've found this discussion very…useful.'

'I thought you didn't like that word.'

'That depends on the context.' She shrugged and wound a curl around her finger. 'Understanding what makes someone tick is always useful, Rocco. It helps me make some kind of sense out of what happened.'

And then she smiled and inexplicably Rocco felt his heart pound and for a moment he found himself wishing he'd kept his mouth shut and that they could just have spent the day in bed. 'Let's go,' he said abruptly.

CHAPTER EIGHT

THEY SAT BENEATH a canopy of tangled green leaves as the Mediterranean sea glittered in a blue haze in front of them. The waiter had just brushed away the remains of the seafood platter but Nicole could see a shiny pink piece of prawn shell he must have missed, which sat on the tablecloth like a picked-off piece of nail varnish. She leaned back in her chair, knowing she couldn't keep staring at the table or distracting herself with the amazing view for much longer. Wishing there were somewhere else to look than at Rocco's ruggedly handsome face.

Yet there was nowhere else she would rather look. She could have feasted her eyes on him all day—on those fiercely intelligent eyes and lips which smiled so rarely, but, when they did, it was like the sun coming out from behind dark cloud. She wondered what he was trying to do to her. To beguile her with a glimpse of how life could have been as his wife, if he'd loved her rather than being programmed to hurt her?

Today they had played tourist in his adopted city where he'd shown her the Monaco which was hidden behind the façade of glitzy shops, exploring narrow streets which felt as if they were full of secrets. They walked through the beautiful Saint Martin gardens and the Byzantine cathedral and the Place du Palais, where they joined all the other sightseers watching the daily changing of the guard. Side by side they stood, their bodies close but never quite touching while Nicole's skin tingled with unwilling frustration.

And they'd ended up in this beautiful restaurant where the waiter had just placed two leather menus in front of them and Rocco was still studying her with those mesmerising eyes, which spoke of his distant Greek ancestry.

'Would you like dessert?'

She shook her head. 'Not really. How about you?'

His gaze became speculative. 'What I want isn't on the menu.'

'You want them to make you something special?'

'Like what?'

She opened her eyes very wide because suddenly she realised they were flirting. 'Oh, I don't know—a soufflé maybe, or some *crepes suzette*?'

He leaned forward and lowered his voice, even though nobody could possibly overhear them. 'After what we were doing last night, I'm amazed you can ask those questions with such an innocent look on your face,' he said. 'Which makes me wonder whether it's real or whether it's feigned. Or whether it's an invitation for me to acknowledge the heat which has been building between us all morning and won't seem to go away. Is that what you'd really like me to do, Nicole?'

She met his gaze before turning her head away, afraid of what he might be able to read in her eyes, when she didn't even want to admit it herself. 'I don't know what I want,' she confessed.

'Then perhaps I will make the decision for us. I think we ought to discuss this matter further, only in private.' His words filtered over her skin. 'So why don't we leave the table and do just that?'

The sudden tightness in Nicole's chest was making it very difficult to breathe. 'You mean...you want to go back to the house?' she croaked.

He shook his head. 'No. That's not what I mean. Who wants to waste time trailing back through the city?'

'Well, what, then?'

'We could get a room.'

'Where?'

'Right here. This restaurant serves some of the best food in the city, but it also has rooms.' He paused as he looked at her. 'But you might not want that.'

Nicole shifted uncomfortably beneath his searching expression. Of course she *wanted* to. She'd wanted nothing else since they'd left his house that morning when the world had seemed to blur so that Rocco had become her only real focus, no matter how detached she had been when studying the architecture of the city or how many paintings she'd looked at. When just having him that near had been like electricity firing over her skin—making her long for them to get properly close. She'd told herself sex wasn't going to happen again. That she'd emerged from that passionate bout last night with her heart just about intact and she wasn't sure she'd be so lucky if there was a next time.

But her body was hungry and her desire was strong—and maybe Rocco had picked up on that. She licked her lips, trying not to be affected by his raven-dark glint of his hair in the sunshine, or the pure muscular power of his body. If she was being sensible she would say no. She would suggest he call for the bill and take her back to the house while she whiled away a few blameless hours by the pool, before getting ready for cocktails on his yacht. She would play at being his wife in public and for the rest of the time she would do her best to avoid him, just as she'd originally planned.

But being sensible wasn't all it was cracked up to be. When was the last time she'd been *reckless*? When she'd thought about what she really *wanted* rather than what she needed? Next week she would be back in Cornwall with damp clay underneath her fingernails and bills to pay, but today she was on a sunny Mediterranean terrace and the only man she had ever really wanted was asking her to go to bed with him. Surely only a fool would turn down an opportunity like that.

'They might not have a room,' she said.

His eyes gleamed. 'We could try.'

Of course, they *did* have a room and Nicole felt like a naughty schoolgirl as Rocco handed over his credit card and was given a key. And crazily, she found herself wishing she were wearing her wedding band, which was the only piece of jewellery she'd kept from her marriage. She wondered what the staff thought of customers who came for lunch, then booked themselves a room. Did they think she was Rocco's mistress and he was about to spend an illicit afternoon with a woman who wasn't his wife? And wasn't it ironic that somehow she seemed to fit that role much better? She'd made a much better mistress than she had a wife, she reflected.

The ride in the elevator was conducted in a breathless kind of silence, mainly because of the presence of a middle-aged woman who was decked in diamonds and carrying a small white dog in her handbag. But Nicole honestly didn't think she would have dared go anywhere near Rocco even if the elevator had been empty. She was in such a heightened state of excitement that she suspected a single touch would have had her clawing at him like a wildcat. Greedily taking what she could from him in the certain knowledge that after Sunday she would be saying goodbye for ever.

After what felt like an eternity, the lift came to a halt and Rocco swiped the key card with a hand which wasn't quite steady. Their room was opulent, with silken drapes and Persian rugs. The walls were decorated in soft shades of grey and the air heavily scented with freshly cut crimson roses. But the décor was nothing but a secondary feature because the moment the door closed behind them, they started pulling at each other's clothes.

'Rocco…be careful,' she breathed as he tugged impatiently at the zip of her sundress. 'If you tear it, I don't have anything else to wear—'

'Then I'll send out for a replacement,' he drawled as the white dress pooled to her ankles and he briefly lifted her up so she was free of it. 'There are plenty of shops close by.'

It was an arrogant assertion and Nicole's heart sank as she acknowledged that this was the way he operated. You ripped a woman's dress off and then you bought another. And she realised something else, too. That whatever his love-life had been since their marriage ended—Rocco wouldn't stay celibate forever. Of course he wouldn't. One day he would be renting a post-lunch room with someone else like this and ripping off *her* dress.

But that uncomfortable realisation was banished by the practised touch of his fingers as they skated over her quivering flesh. With one-handed dexterity he unclipped her bra and let the lacy garment fall to the ground, his lips immediately locking around her nipple and making her moan softly. He was undoing the belt of his trousers as Nicole began unbuttoning his shirt, her fingers sliding eagerly over the silken warmth of his bare chest. The only sound she could hear was the growing intensity of their laboured breathing until the final piece of clothing was removed and they were both naked.

Impatiently, he threw aside the silken cushions and laid her on top of the bed, stretching her arms above her head as if she were some kind of ancient sacrifice. And didn't it feel a bit like that, as he licked at her nipples before turning his attention to the hollow of her navel? It felt primitive and exciting and somehow *inevitable*. Nicole held her breath as his tongue traced a sinuous path to her parted thighs, at last flickering over the gloriously aroused bud until she was brokenly pleading for him to stop teasing her. She wanted him. All of him. She wanted him *inside* her.

'Can't you wait, *piccolo*?'

'No!' she gasped.

'So I see.' His laugh was low and exultant as he stroked on a condom and his hard body came down on top of hers.

'Rocco!' she moaned, tilting her hips towards him, and suddenly he was making that first deep thrust which filled her and the lips she'd opened to cry out her pleasure were being silenced by the hungry pressure of his kiss.

Nicole had never experienced anything quite so intense. Was that because for the first time she *really* felt like his equal—a lover who knew how to please him? Who could meet him on his own terms instead of being the unlikely mistress or the doormat wife? Her head thrashed wildly against the pillow as he drove into her and very quickly tipped her over the edge. Her body started convulsing and almost immediately she felt Rocco bucking inside her as he gave that shuddered groan she recognised so well. His body warm and spent, he collapsed against her, his heart pounding against her damp breasts, and her fingertips automatically moved up to stroke the ruffled tendrils of his hair.

In silence they lay there and must have fallen asleep, because when Nicole's eyes eventually flickered open it was to find her lips pressed against Rocco's neck. The tip of her tongue edged out so that she could taste the saltiness of his damp skin. If only they could stay like this for ever, she thought dreamily. If only all the stuff which had kept them apart didn't exist. But it did. Because this was sex. Nothing but sex. He hadn't dressed it up or cloaked it in promises. He'd booked a room and she'd gone there willingly. And if at this moment they were equals—then maybe she should capitalise on that. Because they hadn't quite finished that conversation of earlier, had they?

'Rocco,' she said, her finger tracing a slow path along the darkened stubble at his jaw.

'Mmm?'

'Can I ask you something else?'

There was a trace of post-coital indulgence in his voice but also the merest note of warning. 'If I say no, will that stop you?'

'No.'

'I didn't think so.' He rolled away from her. 'So what is it now, Nicole?'

If only she'd had time to prepare—like when you went to see the doctor and were supposed to write down all your symptoms on a piece of paper in case you forgot them. As it was, the words came stumbling out in an unplanned rush. 'When you told me earlier that you are the kind of man who hurts women, I wondered… well…' She stared at the stillness of his profile. 'Do you know why?'

'I don't hurt *them*,' he corrected, his voice growing cool. 'I am simply unable to meet their expectations, which are always predictable.'

She arched her brows but deep down she knew what was coming. 'Oh?'

'Women want love,' he said softly. 'And I don't do love.'

'Why not?'

He flexed and unflexed his fingers, the burnished skin looking very dark against the rumpled white sheet.

'Because I can't,' he said at last. 'I'm like someone who was born with no sense of smell—wave a rose underneath my nose and you'd be wasting your time. I don't feel the stuff which other people claim to feel. That's just the way it is. Blame it on the way I was brought up, if you like. Perhaps you have to witness something in order to experience it and there was no real love in our house—at least, not between my parents. Their marriage was based on duty, rather than joy.'

'I see,' said Nicole slowly, trying to absorb what he'd told her. Had he fallen into a familiar pattern when he'd married her, because that too was based on duty? Was that why he'd written her those letters insisting she came back—because he'd felt he *had* to? 'So they weren't happy?'

'Not with each other, no.'

'But they never considered divorce?'

'With three children to consider?' Rocco's mouth hardened. 'No way. And divorce at that time would have been frowned on, especially in that part of Sicily. I guess all their simmering resentment had nowhere to go and was one of the reasons why they lived life so dangerously.'

She shifted her weight slightly, so that she was propping herself up on her elbow. 'What do you mean, *dangerously*?'

He turned to look at her and Nicole thought she caught a flash of vulnerability in his eyes, but it was gone so quickly she might have imagined it.

'They got their kicks out of high-risk stuff,' he said. 'I gather it's a guilt-free way of getting your adrenal buzz, rather than breaking your marriage vows. They opted for dangerous sports rather than infidelity. You know, the kind of activities which make your insurance premiums shoot up. Sky-diving, heli-skiing, free-diving—you name it, they did it. When my father crashed the speedboat it was profoundly shocking but, on some level, I realised I'd been waiting for something like that to happen for a long time.'

Nicole held her breath, unwilling to say anything which might shatter the fragile atmosphere. She wondered why he'd never told her any of this before. *Because they'd never had that kind of relationship.* They'd been about to split up when she'd discovered she was pregnant—and after that, everything had been about the baby. Even after their marriage they'd never confided in one another because their compartmentalised lives had never seemed to overlap. It was only now, when their relationship was almost over, that Rocco seemed prepared to reveal something of the real man behind the successful mask he presented to the world. Too little, too late, she thought—but that didn't stop Nicole's heart from going out to him.

'Oh, Rocco,' she whispered. 'I'm so sorry.'

His voice was dismissive. 'I don't want your pity.'

'It isn't *pity*. It's compassion.'

'Whatever you call it, I don't want it. It all happened a long time ago and I think we've done this subject to death, don't you?' He stifled a yawn and glanced at his watch. 'We'd better order a car to pick us up.'

Nicole registered the dismissive note in his voice and realised what he was trying to do. He was deliberately changing the subject. Telling her in no uncertain terms to keep her pity and her comfort to herself, but Nicole wasn't done. Not yet. She licked her lips. 'Just one more question.'

This time he made no attempt to hide his impatience. 'This is getting tedious, Nicole.'

'I need to know something else, Rocco, and this may be the last chance I get to ask it. Was salvaging your personal reputation the real reason you brought me out here?'

In the muted grey light of the upmarket room, his sapphire eyes looked very startling. 'I could probably swing the deal without you by my side,' he said slowly. 'Let's just say your presence was a precautionary measure.'

'And that's all?'

His eyes met hers. 'Originally.'

'And then?'

He shrugged. 'Once you got out here I realised there was something unfinished between us.'

Her heart pounded. 'You mean sex?'

There was a pause before he nodded. '*Se*. That's exactly what I mean. It has been a long time since I've been intimate with a woman.' He met the question in her eyes. 'Not since the last time I had sex with you, if you're interested.'

'I'm not,' she said breathlessly, and wondered if he could read the lie in her voice.

'It seemed a pity to deny something we both wanted,'

he continued thoughtfully. 'You were always the best lover I'd ever had and I wanted to know if you were as good as I remembered.' He gave an odd kind of laugh. 'And you are. But that's all it was—lust, fired by curiosity.'

'You certainly don't pull your punches, do you, Rocco?'

'Don't ask questions if you can't deal with the answers,' he said as she got out of bed and turned her back on him.

But as he watched her getting dressed, Rocco was aware of a sudden feeling of frustration. He'd thought sex would mean closure—a satisfying finale to their doomed marriage. Yet somehow it hadn't worked out like that. It had ended up being about more than the physical. It had given her the courage to ask him stuff and her questions had made him open up. Made him tell her things. *Feel* things. Things he didn't want to feel. His mouth hardened as he reached down the side of the bed for his phone, closing his eyes to blot out the sight of Nicole pulling a pair of white panties up over her smooth, pale thighs.

Nicole hooked her bra in place, trying very hard to stop her hands from trembling and trying to ignore the fact that Rocco was speaking in rapid French on his phone and acting as if she wasn't even there. She felt like some kind of hooker he'd brought to an anonymous hotel room, and even the revelation that there had been no other woman since their split wasn't enough to calm her ruffled senses. She had been a fool. No two ways about it. She had been there for the taking and he had taken her. His *unfinished business*, as he had described it.

But for her?

For her it felt as if he'd picked her apart and left all the ends unravelled, so that she was left aching and wanting more. Pulling on her white sundress, she tried to smooth out some of the creases. More of him. Why hadn't she realised that physical intimacy would take her to a place where it wasn't safe to go? All that hard work she'd done on herself to try and forget him was all for nothing because right now she felt as vulnerable around Rocco as she'd ever been.

And she still had to endure some wretched cocktail party on his fancy yacht.

Nicole's cheeks were burning as she walked through the lobby in her crumpled white sundress, aware of the doorman's faint and knowing smile. And as she stepped out onto the sun-drenched pavement she realised that Rocco still hadn't kissed her.

CHAPTER NINE

SMALL WAVES SLAPPED rhythmically against the side of the craft and, on the shoreline, distant lights glittered like scattered diamonds. Standing on the deck of his luxury yacht, Rocco Barberi surveyed the guests who were drinking champagne and chattering, wondering why he felt like a spectator at his own party. Fresh oysters and tiny blinis heaped with caviar were doing the rounds, and below deck one of the dealers from the famous nearby casino was demonstrating card tricks to accompanying squeals of disbelief. The party had the indefinable buzz of being a success—and Rocco had just been presented with the succulent cherry which would sit on top of the cake.

A short while ago, Marcel Dupois had taken him aside to say they were satisfied with his offer for the company, and saw no reason for any further delay. Rocco sensed that a deal could be concluded as early as next week and he should have been toasting his own success and looking hungrily to the future, just as he always did.

So why was he feeling a distinct lack of enthusiasm about putting together a new deal?

Why the hell was his temper feeling so damned *frayed*?

He knew why. The evidence was right there before his eyes. Nicole, wearing a close-fitting scarlet dress—a colour he'd never seen her in before—which apparently she'd made herself, just as she'd made the white sundress he'd torn from her body earlier that day. A Nicole who once again had everyone eating out of her hand with a sunny display which was in marked contrast to her distinctly cool mood once they'd left their hotel room.

Had she been angry with him for being so frank with her this afternoon? Her chilly attitude towards him had seemed to suggest as much. As soon as they'd arrived back at his house she had excused herself, saying she needed to get ready—and during the drive here she'd spent the whole time playing with her mobile phone, and acting as if he weren't there.

Yet the moment they'd set foot on his yacht she had blossomed into the vivacious beauty who was drawing the eye of everyone at the party. Heads turned as she walked by and he found himself wondering if people could detect her natural sensuality, as if what they'd been doing straight after lunch was manifesting itself in her glowing appearance. His fingers tightened around the rail, because now he was bitterly regretting having told her things. Things about his parents. About not knowing about love. Things she didn't need to know.

Annelise Dupois was tapping him on the arm. 'Oh, but she is so *charmant*,' she said, her gaze following the direction of his to where Nicole was standing, her mahogany curls illuminated by a soft golden light overhead so that she looked like a dark angel. 'My husband and I were just saying what a lucky man you are, Rocco.'

And for once in his life, Rocco couldn't think of a thing to say. Was it *lucky* that Nicole had somehow acquired the power to make him feel stuff he had no desire to feel? His mouth hardened.

'I understand you and your wife have been estranged?' Javier Estrada chose just that moment to break into his thoughts—the Argentine's apparently innocent question belied by the spark of interest in his black eyes, which was setting Rocco's teeth on edge. He knew the South American tycoon's reputation as a ruthless womaniser and had no intention of giving him the green light where Nicole was concerned. Things might be almost over for them, but he was damned if he would stand by and let a man like Estrada salivate all over her.

'Not any more. We are in the process of reconciliation,' Rocco answered coldly, not caring that it was a lie.

'Pity,' murmured Estrada, and it was as much as Rocco could do not to have him ejected from the boat. Better still, to heave him into the dark waters himself!

But he strode away from him just as a pretty waitress extended her tray of champagne and Rocco waved an impatient hand. He didn't want food, or drink, or to dance to the sound of the string quartet which was entertaining people at the far end of the vast deck. All he seemed capable of doing was thinking about the woman he had married and wondering if he'd taken a temporary leave of his senses when he'd demanded she accompany him this weekend.

He hadn't expected her to be so…

He shook his head. That was the trouble. He had entertained zero expectations where Nicole was concerned. Even when he'd discovered that his desire for her was as potent as before, he'd thought some long-overdue sex was all he needed. It had seemed a simple solution to vent his frustration and get the wife who had deserted him out of his system—all in one neat swoop. His mouth twisted. It just didn't seem to be working out that way. He wondered how he could have made such a bad call and how this whole weekend could have turned into something else. Something he hadn't bargained for. He felt as if Nicole was stripping away layers of himself, leaving him raw and revealing a side he'd always kept hidden. How had that even happened? he asked himself furiously. But really, he knew.

He stared at the dark rippling waves of the sea. It was because Nicole had changed. She was no longer that uncertain woman who gazed at him with reproachful eyes and was prepared to take whatever he dished out. This new version was more sure of herself. Confident and self-assured, she was behaving as if leaving their marriage had given her the courage to be herself. As if *he* had been holding her back.

His mouth hardened. Well, let her think whatever she wanted to think. Soon she would be gone and out of his mind. In the morning he would put her on a flight back to England and sign the divorce papers and that would be it.

The end.

He watched as Anna Rivers walked by in a strappy

little silver gown—the actress slanting him a slow and lazy smile over her shoulder as she passed. Despite having discovered his marital status, the invitation in her eyes was unmistakable but Rocco wasn't interested. He scowled. He'd had enough of women for the time being. Once Nicole had gone and the dust had settled he would resume the life he'd had before she'd tumbled into it. He would operate on a level he was comfortable with. Casual affairs with women who knew the score. Women with careers and lives of their own, who he could take or leave as it suited him. Not women who tried to burrow underneath his skin and stay there.

As soon as they left the cocktail party he would say goodnight and in the morning he would have left for the office long before she awoke. And despite the fact that she was undoubtedly the sexiest woman at the party, he would not share her bed or her body tonight. It was too disquieting. Too...*intense*. That way she had of cooing in his ear when he was deep inside her. The soft wrap of her thighs around his back while he rode her. He felt the warm wash of hunger heating his blood but, deliberately, he dampened it down. Bringing her here had been a mistake, he conceded grimly. A mistake he would not compound by being intimate with her again.

The phone in his pocket began to vibrate and he glanced at it, his senses instantly on alert when he saw it was a missed call from Sicily. And it was late. Was it his grandfather? he wondered, his heart clenching with instinctive dread as he followed the sway of Anna River's bottom towards the lower deck. But once there, he bypassed the actress's footsteps to turn left, heading for the sanctuary of his on-board office before putting a call through to the Barberi complex, just outside Palermo.

Maria answered the phone on the first ring—not a good sign—and Rocco automatically slipped into dialect to speak to the family's housekeeper.

'Nonno?' he demanded.

'Your grandfather is sick,' said Maria.

'How sick?'

'He has a fever. Some kind of infection, the doctor says. We called him straight away.'

Rocco's fingers tightened around the phone. 'And what's happening now?'

'He is on medication and we have hired a nurse. She's with him now. So am I.' There was a pause. 'Are you coming home, Rocco?'

'Of course I'm coming home!'

There was another pause and this time Rocco was certain he could hear the voice of his grandfather in the background—weaker than he'd ever heard him speak before. 'Is that Nonno?' he demanded. 'What's he saying?'

Maria's next words were tentative. 'He wants to know if you are reconciled with your wife.'

Rocco narrowed his eyes. *'What?'*

'Michele mentioned that Nicole has been staying with you in Monaco,' said Maria.

Silently, Rocco swore. What right did his assistant have to go informing on him to his family, like some sort of amateur spy? He would have words with her, he thought grimly—but that would have to wait.

'He wants you to answer his question,' Maria said. 'And you know he will not rest until you do so.'

Rocco stared around his on-board office without really seeing it. If it had been anyone other than his grandfather he would have told them to go to hell. But Nonno was different. He had a place in Rocco's life which nobody else could ever occupy. He had been there for him and his siblings when their world had imploded. He had been the one true rock in their world. And he might be dying. Pain shot through him and Rocco's eyes refocussed as slowly he became aware of his surroundings—the fancy office from which he had conducted some of his most audacious deals. Yet all the gleaming wood and brass might as well have been muddy pieces of driftwood. Suddenly all the awards and commendations counted for nothing.

Niente.

Because these were not the things which mattered.

'No,' said Rocco, aware that his voice was husky with fear. 'We are not reconciled.'

His words were now being conveyed to Nonno but Rocco didn't need Maria to come back on the line to tell him what he could hear for himself.

'He wants to see her, Rocco. He wants you to bring her to Sicily.'

The party was in full swing and Nicole was trying very hard to listen to what the tall Frenchman with the purple bow tie was saying. She knew he was a shareholder and that they viewed Rocco's bid very favourably. She knew that because he'd told her, even though he probably shouldn't have done—but he, like everyone else, seemed to be knocking back the expensive champagne which was being served as freely as water. But it was difficult to concentrate on his words. Difficult to think about anything other than the fact that Anna Rivers had just left the deck with Rocco following the beautiful actress, and that he had been gone for some time.

Nicole told herself it didn't matter where he went or who he went with, but that wasn't quite true. She was suddenly finding that it mattered a lot more than it should have done, yet that was stupid. Just because she'd had hot sex with him that afternoon didn't mean she had any rights over him. Hot sex when he *hadn't even kissed her*. That told her pretty much what he really felt about her, didn't it?

Her cheeks were flushed as she walked to the far end of the deck where it was much quieter. Did Rocco realise that the takeover bid was pretty much a done deal? Had he now decided she was surplus to requirements and he could safely ignore her for most of the party? Probably. What did she expect? That he would treat her with respect when she'd behaved that way—falling into his arms as if none of the bad stuff had happened?

There was a buzz behind her and Nicole turned to see Rocco reappear, looking dramatically handsome in his dinner suit, his black hair gleaming beneath the coloured fairy lights which were strung around the deck. He was looking around, as if trying to locate someone, and then he saw her and began to walk towards her. But the instinctive leap of her heart was replaced by a distinct sense of foreboding as she saw the ravaged look which was darkening his features.

'What's wrong?' she said as soon as he'd reached her.

'I've just had a call from Sicily.' His jaw clenched. 'My grandfather is sick.'

Nicole sucked in a breath, her shock much greater than it should have been because Turi was very old and so such news could never be described as unexpected. But some people seemed indestructible and the elderly patriarch was one of them. She tried to imagine the Barberi complex without the larger-than-life figure at its helm and couldn't. She wondered how it would be for Rocco and his siblings if they lost the man who had always been there for them. The lynchpin of their lives. She looked up into Rocco's empty eyes. 'I'm so sorry,' she said. 'How…how bad is it?'

He shrugged. 'They don't know. My brother is in South America and my sister has been in Los Angeles, so everyone is away. They're both on their way home, but the flights are long and he needs someone with him now. I'm going to Sicily as soon as air traffic control have approved my flight plans. Michele is sorting that out for me now.'

'Yes, of course.' Briefly, Nicole closed her eyes, praying that Rocco would reach his grandfather in time, but she couldn't prevent the other thought which came rushing through her mind. That this really was the last time she would ever see him. She opened her eyes, unprepared for the cold wash of heartache which followed in the wake of this realisation. This really *was* goodbye, she thought, and was just working out how best to say it, when Rocco spoke again.

'He wants to see you, Nicole.'

She blinked, aware that his shadowed eyes had grown flinty and a muscle was working insistently at his temple. 'Who does?' she said.

'Nonno. I spoke with Maria. He's been asking for you.'

'For me?' She didn't make any attempt to hide her bewilderment because there had been no real closeness between her and the octogenarian patriarch, no matter how hard she had tried. 'But why?'

'Who knows?' he growled, tugging impatiently at his tie as if it were strangling him. 'Turi is a law unto himself and always has been.' There was a pause. 'Will you come, Nic?'

'Do you want me to come?' she questioned quietly, trying not to react to a nickname he hadn't used in a long, long time.

He seemed to steel himself before shaking his head. 'Not really,' he said. 'I think we both know that you and I have reached the end of the line. But my grandfather could die at any moment—and who am I to deny a dying man his wish?' He looked her straight in the eyes and they might as well have been alone in a room, rather than on a crowded yacht in the middle of a cocktail party.

Nicole met his questioning gaze. Nobody could accuse Rocco of lying—or caring how much his words could hurt. Yet behind his blunt statement she could sense a vulnerability which for once he wasn't bothering to hide. Maybe he couldn't hide it. Suddenly it occurred to her that right now Rocco needed her as she'd always wanted to be needed by him, but like everything else it had come too late.

And she was scared. Going back to Sicily had the potential to reopen painful wounds—but what choice did she have? If she had any kind of conscience she couldn't refuse what he was asking of her. She was doing this for a sick man, yes, but she was also doing it for Rocco— because she could never live with herself if she let him down. And how crazy was that? 'Of course I'll come,' she said quietly.

'*Grazie.*' He nodded, before glancing down at her red dress. 'We need to go straight from here to the airfield. There won't be time to return to the house but I can get Michele to pack your clothes and have them sent straight to the plane.'

'That's fine,' she said.

'Then let's get going,' he said roughly.

Silently, they slipped away from the party and Nicole could see people smiling as they passed. Were they assuming that she and the Sicilian were sneaking away to celebrate the impending deal, or maybe the renewal of their own relationship?

And for one brief moment, didn't some rogue part of her wish it *had* been a real reconciliation instead of a cold-blooded arrangement to settle some *unfinished business*? Instead, she risked getting herself in even deeper than before, by agreeing to return to a place full of difficult memories—a place where she had been nothing more than an outsider. Would Rocco remember that and look out for her or would he simply throw her to the lions, the way he'd done before?

A hundred questions were bubbling up inside her and she stole a glance at Rocco as his private jet soared up into the starlit skies over Monaco, wondering if she should just be upfront and ask them. But his profile was hard and uncompromising and, sensing he had little appetite for conversation, or any more of her unwanted questions, Nicole spent the flight in an uneasy silence.

CHAPTER TEN

It was dark when Rocco's jet landed in Sicily and the air was as deeply scented as Nicole remembered. She breathed it in with remembered clarity, her senses saturated by the fragrance of lemon and jasmine, and earth baked warm by the sun. She thought how peculiar it was that the stars on this island always seemed brighter than they did anywhere else, or maybe it was just that the sky was darker.

Suddenly a whole shoal of memories began to bombard her. Memories which had the power to make her heart twist with regret. The way she'd felt about Rocco when he'd brought her here. The way he'd kissed her and told her that he would try to be the best father he could. The way she'd lain in his arms and imagined a future for them with their baby. She shook her head a little, surprised by the sudden yearning which washed over her. Was it self-protection which had made her forget all the positive stuff about their marriage, hoping that would make it easier to forget him?

She walked down the aircraft steps where a car was waiting, with a driver Nicole recognised sitting behind the wheel. He gave her a brief nod of acknowledgment, and as he and Rocco slipped naturally into dialect Nicole turned to look out of the window as they drove through the darkened Sicilian countryside.

She stared at the olive trees which lined the roads, their leaves metallic as they glinted beneath the moonlight, their fruits tiny and as yet unripened. The countryside looked unfamiliar in the darkness but the sprawling Barberi residence was exactly as she remembered. As the electronic gates swung open Nicole could see the various residences laid out before her, and the lateness of the hour would have normally ensured that the main house was dark and silent. But the lights blazing from the windows indicated that things were far from 'normal'.

Rocco turned to her as soundlessly the car slid to a halt in the forecourt, his features shadowed. 'Why don't you make your way to our house and get settled in?'

She nodded. 'Okay.'

"I'll go straight to Turi. If you want anything to eat or drink, Maria will still be up.'

Was that a flash of fear she could read in his eyes as he pushed open the car door? The fear of confronting the mortality of someone you loved? Impulsively, she reached across for his hand and squeezed it and for a moment Rocco stilled before squeezing hers back. And Nicole thought how strange it was that such a small gesture could somehow seem more intimate than sex itself.

'Send Turi my love,' she said huskily.

'I will.'

Carrying her small suitcase, Nicole made her way

across the terrace towards the house where she and Rocco had begun and ended their married life. Security lights flickered on and illuminated the imposing building in a golden halo of light. *Our house*, Rocco had said, but it had never really been her house, had it? And it had certainly never felt like home. It had been filled with dark antique furniture which had been in the Barberi family for many decades, and she'd found the style heavy and oppressive but had been too timid to suggest any changes. Too timid to do anything really, except feel eternally grateful that Rocco hadn't kicked her out on the street when she'd fallen pregnant.

Pushing open the door, she clicked on the lights and began to reacquaint herself with the place, trying to get herself into a state of calm to face whatever lay ahead. It was all exactly as she remembered. Only the room they'd designated as a nursery had altered. The crib had gone and so had that swirly animal mobile which she'd brought with her from England. Everything gone. The walls were painted a neutral colour instead of that sunny yellow, and, although it was furnished with a couple of comfortable armchairs and a sophisticated sound system, it didn't look like a room anyone had ever used. Because Rocco didn't live here any more, she reminded herself fiercely. And he'd never even told her why he'd left.

She went to the bathroom, stripped off her red dress and took a long shower—the soapy water sluicing off her heated skin making her feel relatively human again. Afterwards she raided her suitcase for the T-shirt which doubled as a nightshirt and slipped it on. She found some cold water in the fridge and drank it and thought maybe she should stay awake in case Rocco came back. But she was tired. Bone-tired. So much had happened in such a short time. Perhaps she would just lie down and wait.

Unable to face the master bedroom, she grabbed a blanket and lay on one of the sofas in the sitting room, yawning heavily and trying to keep her heavy eyelids open. But Rocco didn't return and the minutes ticked by—and next thing she knew she could feel the warmth of the morning sun on her face. Blinking, she scrambled off the sofa. She'd left the shutters open and she gazed out at the Sicilian morning. Already, the sky was a deep and cloudless blue and in the distance she could hear the sound of church bells. The birds were singing like crazy and the sheer beauty of the morning inexplicably bolstered her spirits. She found her case and she put on jeans and a T-shirt. As she brushed her curls she thought about Turi and offered up a silent prayer that he'd made it through the night.

It would have been easier to go into the kitchen to see if there was any coffee but Nicole knew she couldn't keep putting off going into the room she'd never thought she would see again. Her pulse was skittering against her wrists as she walked into the bedroom she'd shared with Rocco—an elegant room dominated by a huge antique bed. She remembered how gentle he'd been with her. So protective of the new life inside her. Only now could she understand the reason for the exaggerated delicacy with which he'd handled her, when at the time she'd feared he now longer found her attractive. It was strange the perspective which distance gave you.

Swallowing down the sudden lump in her throat, she looked around. On one of the walls was her only contribution to the décor—a black and white photograph of New York, which she'd admired on their honeymoon and which Rocco had secretly bought and had shipped here, so it was waiting for her on their return. She remembered being overwhelmed by the gesture, thinking it symbolised a romantic future which hadn't ever materialised. And it twisted her heart with nostalgia as she stared at it. Why was it still hanging there?

She wasn't sure what made her open the closet but what she found inside unsettled her even more than the picture had done. Because all her clothes were there— exactly as she'd left them. Neat lines of colour-coordinated outfits which had been chosen by the expensive London stylist. Shirtdresses and neat trousers—all with toning shoes and accessories. Yet looking at them now she could see that, although they weren't her style, they were in no way offensive. Why had she made such a fuss about them?

She sighed. The problem hadn't been in the choice of clothes, but in her. If you let people treat you like a doll then you couldn't really complain when they did, could you? She wondered, if she could do it all again, whether she would have behaved differently, but really she knew the answer. Of course she would—but the outcome would probably have been the same. Because a marriage could only work if it was based on love and Rocco didn't have the ability to love—he'd told her that himself.

As if thinking about him had somehow conjured him

up, Rocco chose that moment to walk into the bedroom and Nicole's questions were forgotten as she searched his face, registering eyes which were shadowed from lack of sleep and a hard and unsmiling mouth.

Her heart squeezed. 'Turi?' she questioned, her voice squeaky with anxiety.

His jaw tightened but he nodded. 'He's hanging on in there. He's in some kind of deep sleep. He didn't seem to know I was there.' He paused and a muscle began to work at his temple. 'I don't know if he's well enough to see you right now and—'

'Honestly, Rocco—it doesn't matter.' Her words tumbled over themselves. 'He may not have been himself when he suggested seeing me—and there's your brother and sister to consider. I don't want him exhausted when they arrive and maybe I'd better not—'

'Shh,' he said, and his voice was unexpectedly gentle. 'It's okay. The doctor says that, physically, he's as strong as an ox—and he's been defying the odds all his life. Let's just see how he goes. He wants to see you, Nic—and as far as I'm concerned, that's what's going to happen.'

Nicole nodded, thinking that the things they were saying to each other were polite and functional but there was a whole different conversation going on underneath the surface. At least, for her there was. She looked into Rocco's eyes and wondered what he thought when he saw them both standing here in this bedroom, like ghosts of the people they used to be. Did he find it as poignant as she did? Were the memories flying out of nowhere to remind him that it hadn't been all bad? But these were questions she would never ask because she had no right to.

'I'm going to take a shower,' he said, his hand reaching up to undo the buttons of his shirt. 'And then we'll go over to the main house and have some breakfast. Maria is waiting for us.'

The sight of her husband about to start undressing was enough to have Nicole scuttling from the bedroom and thirty minutes later they were sitting in the kitchen of the main farmhouse, with Maria bustling around them. The housekeeper had been with the Barberi family since Rocco was a baby and greeted Nicole with a surprising affection, enveloping her in a fierce hug which left her breathless. Afterwards she turned and said something in rapid dialect to which Rocco made a drawling response which had Nicole looking at him questioningly.

'She says that Turi's fate is in God's hands now,' Rocco interpreted. 'That he is very frail but she is certain he will recover now that I have returned. And I told her that if she was trying to make me feel guilty about moving to Monaco—then it wasn't going to work.' Unexpectedly, his eyes flashed with humour. 'She also wants to know if you'd like some *granita* with your coffee?'

'I'd love some,' said Nicole, sitting down at the table and taking the bowl which was being pushed towards her.

Rocco watched as Nicole began spooning up the famous Sicilian *granita* which Maria had made using lemons taken from the estate. His grandfather had made it through the night, his brother and sister were on their way and the coffee he was drinking was strong and dark. There were many reasons to count his blessings, but the tension in his body remained as tight as ever. Was it having Nicole here which was disturbing him so much? Sitting across the table from him with her dark curls tumbling over her shoulders and her rosy lips looking so kissable. He put his cup down with a bang, resenting the sudden shafting of his body because surely he shouldn't be feeling desire when his grandfather lay upstairs, so sick.

But it *was* desire, that was the trouble. It was there, ever-present—as much a part of him as the blood which pulsed through his veins. He watched as his wife popped a piece of deep-fried *ciambella* into her mouth and tried not to be distracted by the luscious curves of her breasts pushing against her simple T-shirt. She was simply… captivating and suddenly he found himself wondering what the hell he was going to do with her all day while she was here—if you discounted the very obvious.

A pulse flickered at his temple. Occupying himself wouldn't normally be a problem but this was different. For once Rocco realised he couldn't escape into the endless refuge of work, or allow himself to be consumed by its constant demands. He could hardly leave Nicole to amuse herself while he locked himself in the office, could he? He glanced across at her, mentally sifting through all his options. If he took her to the nearby village or even into Palermo itself—by evening it would be all round the island that Rocco Barberi was back with his wife. And that was not going to happen – because it wasn't true.

'Why don't we go for a walk round the estate?' he said, watching as her benign expression changed into one of wariness. Was she remembering how their walk around the Rock of Monaco had ended, with him hiring a room after lunch—a room blatantly intended for sex? Was that why she produced a distinctly cool smile in response?

'Sure. Why not?'

This time he didn't need to suggest she change her shoes, because her footwear was sensible, and this time there was no sense of showing her somewhere new. Because she knew this place. He didn't have to point out the way when he suggested going to the orchards—she turned left automatically. It had been easy to forget that she'd lived here. Too easy, perhaps.

To Rocco's surprise, the morning unfolded with a surprising sense of effortlessness as Nicole reacquainted herself with the Barberi estate. Her enthusiasm seemed genuine as she admired the terracotta and green landscape and she even remembered the word for goat as she surveyed the rangy-looking creatures who were gnawing away in one of the scrubby meadows. It was when they reached the olive groves and he was congratulating himself on managing to kill a few hours without any kind of drama, when she asked the question he guessed he should have been expecting all along.

'So why exactly did you move to Monaco, Rocco?' she said, her English voice sounding very clear and steady. 'Why leave Sicily when it's clear you love the place so much?'

Rocco took his time before answering, bending down to study one of the rose bushes planted at the end of each line of olive trees, to discourage insects away from the precious fruit. Satisfied with the gardener's efforts, he straightened up, brushing his hands down over his thighs. 'Because most of my work is in mainland Europe and it cut my commuting time right down.'

'And your grandfather didn't...' She lifted her shoulders. 'Didn't he miss you?'

'I'm sure he did,' he drawled. 'But he soon got used to it. People migrate all the time. And my sister lives here. The last thing Turi would want would be for me to stay here out of some kind of duty.'

Rocco's mouth hardened. Because he'd been absolved of duty. He'd done more than his fair share of it and Turi understood that. He glanced at his watch, wanting to put an end to this. To stop the introspection which always seemed to affect him whenever Nicole was around. 'The nurse said you could go in before lunch, even if Nonno's asleep. Shall we go back to the house to get something to drink first?'

She nodded. 'Yes, please. And I'd like to freshen up.'

Back at the house, Rocco took the opportunity to check his emails while Nicole went to change and he was just passing the partially open door of the spare room when a movement from inside made him glance in.

He had automatically thought she'd be using their old bedroom even though he'd noticed earlier that the bed hadn't been slept in last night. But she hadn't. Yet again she had chosen a room away from him, and as he looked in he could see she was struggling with her dress. He saw her hand angling awkwardly down her back as she struggled to pull up the zip and even though he knew it was the wrong thing to do, he found himself standing in the doorway, as if somebody had wound the clock back and he were her husband again. As if he had a right to take part in all those small domestic rituals which were a part of every marriage.

'Can I help?'

She looked up and a flurry of emotions crossed her face. She screwed her nose up, as if something inside her was hurting—and then suddenly she gave an almost efficient nod of agreement. As if she would be a fool to struggle with her own zip when someone was willing to take over the troublesome task for her.

Only it didn't quite happen that way.

Rocco honestly didn't think he had intended seduction at that moment but the instant his fingers connected with her silky flesh, he was lost. Maybe she was, too, because he heard a shuddered sigh escape from her lips. So that suddenly, instead of doing the zip up, he was sliding it down. All the way down to where her back curved inwards and then beyond even that, so that all it needed was the slightest tug of his fingers to let the garment slide to the ground. But he paused before he did that. Long enough to allow her to move away or chastise him and ask him what the hell he thought he was playing at.

But she didn't. Her sigh became a quickened breath

and still she said nothing as he slid his hands around her back to cup her straining breasts. He could feel his erection hard and almost painful as it pressed against her lacy lingerie and he thought maybe it would be better if he did this almost...*anonymously*. He could push her up against that wall and pull her panties down before freeing himself. He could slip inside her from behind. He could take her quickly and efficiently and give them both pleasure and not a single word need be exchanged. They didn't even have to look at one another. And afterwards they could make as if it had never happened. They would never speak of it again. He'd done that with other women before, but never with Nicole.

And he didn't want to do that now. Not with her. Never with her. He gave a little groan as he turned her round to find her eyes as darkened and as full of sensual promise as he'd hoped they would be. He bent to slide his arm beneath her knees and carried her over to the bed.

'I want you,' he said unsteadily as he laid her down on top of the embroidered cover, before ripping the shirt from his body, uncaring of the buttons which broke free.

'And I want you,' she echoed chokingly.

'Nicole—'

But she silenced him with a fierce shake of her wild curls. 'I don't want analysis or promises neither of us can keep,' she said. 'I just want you, Rocco. Now. That's all.'

And wasn't it ironic that by taking *his* line—by removing all the emotion from what was about to happen—

she somehow increased her power over him? So that, for the first time in all the time he'd known her, it felt as if it was *Nic* who was taking charge. As if everything he'd ever taught her had crystallised into this one, single act. It felt as if they were doing it in slow motion. As if their bodies were glued together, with no space between them. He kissed her. And kissed her. His lips brushed over hers in a tantalising graze until hers eagerly parted and he licked his way over their trembling surface.

She gave a gasp as he entered her and he blotted out the sound with the slow caress of his lips. She wrapped her soft thighs around his bare back and he thrust. And thrust again. He made it last for as long as he could, until the little cry she gave sounded as if she might be in some sort of pain, and then he came too and all thought was temporarily banished from his mind.

But her smile was dreamy when he studied her afterwards and he could instantly feel himself hardening again. He leaned over her, his lips automatically seeking hers, but she wriggled away from him with a decisive shake of her head.

'No,' she said.

'Really?'

'Really.'

'Why not?'

'You know exactly why not, Rocco. We shouldn't have done it once—and we're certainly not going to do it twice.'

'Because?'

'Because… There are a million reasons, which you really don't need me to articulate for you, but mainly because I have to go and see your grandfather and the nurse will be expecting me.'

He nodded. 'Okay. Go and take a shower. I'll use one of the other bathrooms and wait for you downstairs.'

Her words echoed round in his mind as Rocco stood beneath the jets of the gushing shower, and he reluctantly realised Nicole had been right. They shouldn't have done it. Because what purpose had it served? Okay, it had fed his desire—and hers—but they were supposed to be over, and divorcing couples didn't keep having sex.

He turned off the shower and towelled himself dry but once he'd dressed and gone downstairs he was surprised by a wave of emotion. He found himself thinking about the future and about what might happen when Turi died. Even if he survived this bout of illness, he couldn't go on for ever. Nobody could. Rocco found himself asking what it was going to be like here once Turi had gone and why he'd never stopped to think about it before.

Because Turi had always been there. A man who was larger than life—and you imagined that those kinds of men never died.

But they did.

He wondered if his siblings would turn to him and expect him to slip into the replacement role of patriarch? What if he told them he wasn't interested in such a role? That he had already given as much as he was prepared to give to ensure the survival of the family?

Was he in danger of overthinking matters because he'd been stirred up by Nicole's presence here? And

wasn't he in danger of allowing her to skew his vision?
Just because the sex had been dynamite, didn't mean it
couldn't be as good with somebody else. His lips hardened with renewed resolve as he heard her light foot-
step on the stairs.

Once she had returned to England everything would
shake down. He could stop looking at his life and questioning it. He could start bedding women who didn't
mess with his head.

He clenched his fists.

Once she had gone.

CHAPTER ELEVEN

'Do you want me to stay?' Rocco questioned as he pushed open the door of the sickroom.

Nicole wasn't sure what she wanted as she stepped into the shuttered room and gazed over at the inert body in the bed. Would Rocco be a comforting presence at her side, or a distraction? The latter, probably—especially after what had just happened back at the house. The sex which had just sort of *happened* and which had blown her away. Not because of his amazing technique, which had never been in question, but because of his unexpected tenderness which had made her heart want to burst with pleasure and break with sorrow, all at the same time. She was just about to politely tell him she'd be fine on her own when the figure in the bed spoke.

'Leave us, Rocco.'

Turi's voice wasn't as strong as Nicole remembered but it still wasn't the kind of voice you ignored and she watched as his grandson gave a terse nod.

'The nurse will be in the room next door, if you need anything,' Rocco said. 'Don't wear yourself out, Nonno.'

Turi lifted a wavering hand to indicate that he should cut short the lecture and leave. 'Come,' the old man said to Nicole, once the door had closed.

Nicole approached the bed. The quietness and the dimness of the room reminded her of nursing her adoptive mother and at that moment she missed Peggy Watson very much. As she grew closer she could see that although age and sickness had diminished him, the faded blue eyes, which must once have been so like Rocco's, were unexpectedly bright as the elderly patriarch gestured for her to sit down.

'Turi,' she whispered as she perched on a chair next to the bed and squeezed his gnarled old hand in hers. 'I wish I could say *I hope you're feeling better*, in dialect.'

'I think we had better speak in English,' he said. 'Don't you?'

Nicole couldn't hide her surprise and something in the way he said it made her suddenly want to get honest with him. Because if you couldn't say what was really on your mind at times like this, then what was the point of anything? She remembered his refusal to use her native tongue when she'd arrived at the house—even rejecting her faltering attempts in Italian as he'd insisted on conversing in Sicilian dialect. 'Unlike before,' she said quietly.

He nodded in agreement. 'That was foolish of me. I recognise that now. I wanted you to integrate fully with life here and I thought that imposing a tough regime from the beginning was the way to do it.' He gave a croaky little sigh. 'I wanted so much, but none of it happened the way it was supposed to. I handled it wrong. Just like I handled Rocco all wrong.'

Nicole felt a frown pleating her brow. 'What do you mean, Nonno? What did you do wrong with Rocco?'

His voice gained more strength as he began to speak. 'Did he ever speak to you of his childhood?'

She shook her head. 'Never. He used to shut all my questions right down and make me feel bad about asking them. It was only very recently that he talked about his parents.'

Turi's eyes were inquisitive. 'You know he was only fourteen when they died?'

She nodded. 'Yes, I knew that much.'

'His brother was nine, his sister only five and the little ones, they were...' The old man blinked his rheumy eyes rapidly. 'They were broken,' he said at last, clearing his throat. 'I was trying to do it all. My wife was no longer alive and I had the business to run—as well as the younger children to cope with. I leaned on Rocco too much. I see that now. I told him...'

Nicole leaned forward as his words faded away. 'What, Nonno? What did you tell him?'

He indicated she should plump up the bank of pillows behind his head, and once she'd done so he lay back on them and continued. 'I told him that the younger children would look to him for strength and that was what he needed to show them. To keep his head down and work hard and carry on, no matter what—because that would hold the family together. To follow my example and never cry or show his feelings. And he didn't. He learned his lesson well. Too well, perhaps.'

To never show his feelings. A painful breath escaped Nicole's lips because didn't Turi's words explain so much about the man she had married? Why he could appear so *distant.* Why he had the ability to bury himself in his work, no matter what was going on around him. Was that why he hadn't reacted as she'd thought he might when she'd had the miscarriage? Why he'd never really talked about it—not even when they'd been having that heart-to-heart in Monaco, when she'd given him every opportunity to do so. 'Yes, he did,' she said slowly. 'But then, I imagine that Rocco must have been an exemplary student in everything he undertook.'

'Not once did I see a tear fall,' Turi added shakily. 'At least, not then.'

Nicole narrowed her eyes as he held her gaze. 'What do you mean?' she whispered. 'Not then?'

There was a pause. 'When *you* left, he was heartbroken.'

Angrily, Nicole shook her head. Turi might be old and sick but even he couldn't convince her of *that.* Heartbroken? Never in a million years. Rocco had pushed her away and no mistake. She remembered him taking a trip to the States when she'd most needed him, weeks after it had happened, when she'd still been mired in her own sense of misery.

But she hadn't told him that, had she? She hadn't really known how and he hadn't seemed to want her to.

She'd put his emotional distance down to the fact that he'd been forced to marry her and once there wasn't going to be a baby, there was no reason for the relationship to continue. Yet what Turi had told her made her look at it differently. Wouldn't Rocco's behaviour be more understandable if he'd been schooled in the art of concealing his true emotions?

No, she told herself fiercely. It wasn't like that. Turi was an old man sentimentalising his past in a clumsy attempt to achieve some sort of peace towards the end of a long life. And she wasn't going to buy into it—because hadn't she already dealt with her own pain? She'd done that and come out the other side and nothing could be gained by dwelling on what could never be. She could allow herself to feel an aching sympathy for the hardships Rocco must have been forced to endure, but she should never start making the mistake of thinking he was capable of loving her, because that way lay madness. He was capable of having fantastic sex with her, as he'd very recently proved—but nothing more than that. 'No,' she said. 'I don't believe you.'

'Yes,' Turi argued, with a sudden vehemence which belied his frail physique. 'What benefit would it bring if I started lying at this stage of my life? Didn't you ask him why he left Sicily? Why he couldn't bear to live in the house once you'd gone? Why he refused to give away any of your things?'

Fear washed over her—a fear which was motivated by stupid, stubborn hope. And hope was futile where Rocco was concerned. Nicole knew that better than anyone. She could see that Turi was looking tired now, as if the exertion of all he'd just told her had exhausted him, and quickly she stood up and poured out a glass of water before holding it to his lips.

'I'm going to go and let you get some rest now,' she said softly.

'Promise me,' he croaked as he took another small sip, then waved the glass away, 'that you will ask him why? Just promise me that, Nicole, even though I have no right to demand such a promise.'

What could she say? How could she possibly refuse a sick man this simple request?

'I promise,' she said, putting the glass down and dropping a light kiss on his forehead, and the old man smiled before his eyes closed.

The nurse must have heard the sound of Nicole's chair scraping against the floor, because the door to the adjoining room opened and she appeared, looking crisp and fresh in her white uniform as she glanced enquiringly at Nicole.

'*Tutto bene, signora?*' she questioned.

Nicole's Italian might have been basic, but even she could understand this simple query. '*Sì. Grazie,*' she said and left the room.

But her head was spinning once she stepped out of Turi's residence with no real idea of what to do or where to go. Buying herself time, she took off to a quiet section of the estate in an attempt to get her thoughts in order, but that proved impossible. She didn't believe Turi because she didn't *want* to believe him. She didn't dare. Because even if what he said was true, what good would come of raking it up now?

Just suppose that Rocco *had* cared for her at the time—he had certainly grown out of it, hadn't he? He'd told her that the only reason he had taken her to Monaco was to have sex with her and get her out of his system and he had done just that. Even an hour ago he had done that. Maybe he would continue having sex with her for as long as she allowed him to and if she did that, wasn't it cheapening what she'd once felt for him?

But she had promised Turi. She'd promised a sick man she would ask Rocco that question. And you couldn't make promises like that and not follow through…

She went to search for him and when Maria informed her he was down among the lemon trees it struck an instant chord. Nicole knew he sometimes liked to take his work there and it had always been one of the prettiest places to sit on the Barberi estate, with its wooden bench placed beneath the sweet scent of the creamy lemon blossom. He had taken her there sometimes when they had returned from their honeymoon, when they would sit quietly listening to the drowsy buzzing of the bees in the lavender bushes, while she'd tried to get her queasy stomach to settle. It had been this place she'd been thinking of when she'd made her bestselling pottery collection.

Her mouth was dry as she approached the lemon grove and saw Rocco sitting beneath the shade of a tree, a weighty-looking sheaf of papers on his lap. The warm sun was beating down on his black hair and he had rolled up the arms of his shirt to reveal his strong forearms. She remembered the way those arms had been holding her just a short while ago. The way his hands had cupped her face as he had kissed her over and over again—as if he couldn't get enough of her kisses.

And hadn't that made her realise…?

No. Not *realise*. That was the wrong word. It had made her *think* she might still be in love with him.

And she wasn't.

She definitely wasn't.

'Rocco?'

He glanced up as she approached, his features darkening as he pushed the papers aside.

'Turi's fine,' she said, in answer to the unspoken question in his eyes. 'The nurse is with him now.' She walked over to the bench and indicated the space beside him. 'Mind if I sit down?'

There was a pause. *'Certo,'* he said, raising his shoulders in a non-committal shrug.

His momentary hesitation jarred, as did the less than welcoming look on his face and Nicole wanted to forget about her promise, but she couldn't. Deliberately choosing the far end of the seat, she sat down, her heart racing as she watched a butterfly hovering over some little white flowers and tried to work out how she could possibly phrase this without looking a complete…

No.

She'd been there and done that. It didn't matter what this did to her reputation or how it made her look. And besides, caring about that kind of thing was shallow. What mattered was getting to the truth, no matter what that might be.

'Turi had some interesting things to say,' she said slowly.

Was there something in her tone which made his face grow guarded? Was that why he slanted her a thought-

ful look which was followed by one of slight *boredom*?
'Do I really want to hear them?' he drawled.

She suspected not, but he was going to hear them
anyway. 'He told me to ask you why you left Sicily. So
I'm asking.'

It was not what Rocco had been expecting and Nicole's words hit him like bullets from a gun. He could
feel his body tensing as every instinct urged him to shut
this topic down. To tell her it was none of her damned
business—nor Turi's either. His laugh was short and, in-
furiatingly, his curiosity stirred. 'No doubt he had a few
ideas himself—a few explanations why that might be?'

She drew in a breath which wasn't quite steady and
he could see the doubt written on her face. 'He did, but
I'm not sure I believed them. He told me lots of things.
He seemed to feel guilty about the way he treated you.'

At this Rocco held up his palm to silence her, wanting her to know that she was in danger of crossing a
forbidden line. 'My grandfather stepped in when my
parents were killed,' he said coldly. 'How could he possibly feel guilty about something like that?'

'That wasn't what I meant,' she persisted. 'He told
me he'd insisted you never show your feelings or emotions after they died. That because you were the oldest
he forced you to be strong for the sake of Olivio and
Romina.'

'And I was damaged as a result? Is that it?' he questioned, before giving a dismissive flick of his hand.
'*Madonna mia*, I had no idea that Turi had taken such an
interest in amateur psychology in his advancing years.'

But Nicole doggedly ignored his sarcasm and kept

her gaze fixed firmly on his. 'So why *did* you leave Sicily?'

He could feel a muscle beginning to work at his temple and once again he wondered how she had the ability to make him feel so damned *angry*. 'Maybe I found it intolerable to stay once my darling wife had disappeared without any warning, leaving the whole of Sicily buzzing and the international press camped out on my doorstep. You can't blame me for wanting to escape all the speculation after you'd gone. And since we're on the subject of raking up the past—just why *did* you go, Nicole?'

'I thought it was what you wanted,' she said dully.

'You thought it was what I wanted?' he repeated. 'Then that just shows how little you really knew me, doesn't it?' He picked up the sheaf of papers as if she were keeping him from something very important and raised his eyebrows. 'Look, I'm grateful to you for coming here and seeing Turi, and I'm glad he's been able to get what was clearly bothering him off his chest since undoubtedly that will aid his recovery, but there isn't any reason for you to stay any longer. We're done here, aren't we? I'll sign the papers and you can have your divorce. My plane will take you back to England as soon as you're ready—and since you're pretty much packed, I don't think there's any reason for you to hang around. *Capisce?*'

The words rolled smoothly from his tongue as if he couldn't wait to get rid of them. To get rid of *her*. Nicole met the sapphire glitter of his eyes. This was her cue to make a dignified exit. To go back to the house and gather her few things together. She would say a rather awkward goodbye to Maria and then be whisked away from here in Rocco's private jet—one last taste of luxury before she returned to her newly single life in England.

Wasn't that what she'd wanted all along?

She could feel the painful pounding of her heart.

No.

It might have been what she'd thought she wanted when she'd first filed those papers, but not any more. Because being with Rocco made her world come alive in a way it didn't do with anyone else, whether she liked it or not. Didn't matter that logic was urging her to get out while she still could, because all the logic in the world couldn't change the fact that her heart ached whenever she was with him. She'd loved him from the start and she loved him still—and love was an emotion which defied logic. She had never known what had made Rocco Barberi the unfathomable man he was, but she did now. She thought how lonely and bewildered he must have been as a bereaved teenager—unable to show his own grief because he was too busy being strong for his siblings. Couldn't she help break down the wall he had built around his heart? Couldn't she try? She'd learnt to articulate her own emotions—maybe she could help him do the same.

Because she didn't want a divorce. She really didn't. She wanted a reconciliation—a real one this time, not one which was just for show. One which might or might not work, but surely they could give it a try.

But only if he wanted it, too.

She sat up very straight, the wooden slats of the bench pressing into her back. 'I don't want to fly back in your private jet, Rocco,' she said in a low voice. 'I want to stay here, with you. Or go back with you to Monaco—whichever you prefer.'

His features darkened. 'What the hell are you talking about?'

He snarled the question rather than asking it and, stupidly, that gave Nicole a glimmer of hope. Because Rocco was cool and measured and controlled, wasn't he? He didn't *snarl*. 'I want to give our marriage another go,' she said calmly. 'And I'm hoping you might feel the same.'

'Are you insane?'

The snarl was even more pronounced now and that gave Nicole the courage to carry on, because now she had nothing left to lose. She was laying it all on the line and pride was pointless. She was fighting for her future, she realised—a future which suddenly seemed empty without Rocco. 'Perhaps a little,' she admitted huskily. 'But I want to tell you a few things I've discovered since you came back into my life.'

'Nicole—'

'Please, Rocco. At least do me the courtesy of hearing me out. Because I've discovered I am as much to blame for what happened as you were,' she said, cutting across his words in a way she would never have dared do before. 'I can see that now. I was just so...*grateful*... that you'd married me. Relieved that I wouldn't end up like my own natural mother—so desperate for money and support that I'd dump my own baby and leave them crying feebly on a snowy hospital step. Only I would never have let that happen,' she added fiercely, flaring her nostrils to suck in a shaky breath. 'No matter what happened, I would have kept our baby…'

Her words tailed off and as she struggled to contain herself, Rocco shifted awkwardly on the seat. 'Nicole,' he said again, only this time his voice sounded almost gentle—like a doctor trying to placate an hysterical patient. 'Please. Don't do this.'

'But I *need* to do it!' she burst out. 'Don't you understand? I wanted you to comfort me after the miscarriage, to tell me that it was all going to be okay and we could try again. After all, lots of women go through that experience. It's not the end of the world, even if it feels like it at the time. But you wouldn't let me near you, Rocco—and I didn't tell you what I wanted. What I needed. I had grown up in so many different foster homes that I never learnt the art of true communication. I learnt to hide my true feelings away because it was safer that way. And like you said, you aren't a mind-reader—how could you have been expected to know what I needed? You were too busy protecting yourself from your own pain. Trying not to show it and succeeding in doing that—as you had been taught to do and have been doing all your life.'

'I don't have to sit here and listen to this,' he said, his blue eyes furious now.

'Oh, I think you do, Rocco. I think this needs to be said, no matter what happens.' She drew in another breath because while this was the hardest thing of all to say, somehow it was the easiest too. 'And I'm telling you that I love you. That I never really stopped loving you. That I'd like the chance to start over. To give our marriage another go—only a real one this time.'

'And you think—what?' He stared at her incredulously. 'That I will magically start to love you, too?'

'Who knows what could happen if you dared let me close?' she whispered. 'Why did you keep all my things if you didn't care about me a little bit? Why didn't you just get rid of them?'

'Did my grandfather tell you to ask me that as well?' he demanded.

Nicole saw his face darken and she realised that she might have pushed him too far. 'He might have mentioned it,' she admitted and then swallowed. 'Look, you don't have to say anything right now. Just think about it, that's all.'

'How confident you sound, Nicole,' he said, and now his words were icy-cold. 'Whatever happened to that wide-eyed amenable woman who first bewitched me?'

'She grew up,' Nicole answered simply. 'And the confidence is just a veneer, Rocco. Inside I'm shaking with nerves because something in my heart is telling me not to just give up on this marriage. So this is what I'm going to do.' For a moment she stared up at the deep blue sky behind the fretwork of leaves and lemon blossom and inhaled the warm, sweet scent of the flowers. 'I'm going to Palermo to find myself a hotel room and to look into the availability of cheap flights back to the UK—'

'And I just told you—'

'I know what you told me and it's a very kind offer

to let me use your plane, but if we're splitting up then I'd rather do it under my own steam. Start as I mean to go on. I'll text you to let you know where I am and which flight I'm booked on, and if you want me to stay…if you're prepared to open up your heart to me, then…' she drew in another breath '…all you have to do is come and get me.'

He rose to his feet, his face darkening as he tucked the sheaf of papers under his arm, his sapphire eyes blazing and brilliant. 'You can have your answer right now, Nicole, and it's very simple. I don't want that kind of relationship. I never did. I'm sorry about everything that's happened but we just have to live with that. Perhaps you were right all along and we need to move on.' One of the sheets of paper he'd been working on fluttered to the ground like an oversized piece of confetti, but he didn't even appear to notice. 'My offer to fly you home remains—but I'm not going to force you onto my plane. It's up to you. Let me know if you change your mind, but that's all you're going to get from me.' His mouth hardened. 'You're on your own from now on.'

CHAPTER TWELVE

THE HOTEL ROOM was small, clean and perfectly functional. It had plain walls, a dark-beamed ceiling and a bed with a mattress so hard it might have been made of stone.

Just like Rocco's heart, Nicole thought before forcing herself to stem *that* particular tide of thought. She couldn't blame him for being the man he was. She couldn't force him to feel emotions he wasn't capable of feeling or make him want to try again. Because that wasn't what he wanted. She'd been honest enough to put her feelings for him on the line and he'd been honest enough to tell her he wasn't interested. All she needed to do now was be grown-up enough to accept the situation *as it was*, not how she wanted it to be.

But, oh, it hurt.

How could it hurt so much?

Because she had allowed him back into her heart, that was why. She'd broken every single promise she'd ever made to herself and now she was paying the price. All those weeks and months and years of trying to forget about her Sicilian tycoon might as well not have happened.

Opening her computer, she went online and booked an early-morning flight for England, then changed and went down to the nearby pizzeria for supper. But despite the delicious smell of the *capricciosa*, she merely prodded at the pizza aimlessly and ate barely any of it. She sat there for a while, drinking coffee, and when at last she left the small restaurant she found herself going into the little church she'd seen at the far end of the street. Stepping into the dimly lit and cool interior, she gazed up at the brightness of the stained glass above the altar and thought about Peggy, and about Rocco's parents, too. She thought of the baby she'd never had, and she lit a candle for all of them. And something in that ageless symbolism gave her a new strength—as if in the flicker of those four flames she saw what she needed to do.

And that was to forget Rocco. To collect her pride and set him free. Her heart pounded. She wasn't going to send him a text telling him which flight she'd be on or which hotel she was staying in because that would be the behaviour of someone desperate, and needy. *And she wasn't that person any more.* She'd told him how she felt but you shouldn't say something just to get something back. Rocco didn't want her—he couldn't have made it any plainer and she needed to get that simple fact into her thick skull. She still had a life and a future—it was just one which didn't involve him. She would go back to Cornwall and make her pots and she wouldn't hide away from what had happened. She would embrace the experience—with all its accompanying pleasure and pain—and produce a new collection based on the things she had seen in Monaco. Who knew? One day she might even be able to think about the man she had married without an aching deep in her heart.

Back in the hotel room she lay beneath the thin sheet, listening to the sounds of people in the street below, as the minutes ticked slowly towards midnight. Her eyes were shadowed from lack of sleep when she woke the next day and she despised the eager way she instantly reached for her phone. But the screen was blank. There was no missed call or message from Rocco asking where the hell she was.

Of course there wasn't. She hadn't told him where she was staying but he did have her mobile number.

How long would it take her to accept that he just didn't want her?

The taxi which took her to the airport next morning was stuffy and smelt of cigarettes and Nicole was glad when she reached the terminal, even though she recognised she was leaving Sicily for ever. And that hurt, too. Wasn't it stupid how everything seemed to hurt today? Half-heartedly she removed her shoes and belt but for once the security process seemed speedy and her progress onto the fully booked flight relatively smooth. She had just snapped on her seat belt when some kind of commotion started happening on the opposite side of the aeroplane. People were pointing out of the windows and exclaiming in voices of rising excitement.

Nicole leaned over to see what they were looking at and her heart gave a lurch of disbelief. Because there, running across the Tarmac like a champion sprinter, was Rocco. Rocco as she'd never seen him before, suddenly appearing breathlessly on the plane, his face filled with dark intensity and something else…something she didn't recognise. He spotted her straight away and began to walk down the central aisle towards her. People's necks were craning and women were turning to watch him as he moved, their voices instinctively murmuring their appreciation.

Sitting bolt upright in her seat, Nicole ignored the loud pounding of her heart and glared at him. How *dared* he do this? Cause some kind of major disruption, which was probably going to get them both into all kinds of trouble. And for *what*? Especially when he'd already rejected her and she'd been coming to terms with that, and now she was going to have to do the same thing all over again.

'What are you doing here?' she bit out.

'You told me you were going to let me know where you were, and you didn't,' he accused. 'I searched every damned hotel in Palermo!'

'Tough. I changed my mind. It's a woman's prerogative—remember? And anyway—you had my number if you wanted me.'

'And if I'd phoned, you probably would have hung up on me.'

How convenient of him to think that. Nicole's lips tightened. 'I probably would,' she agreed steadily, as if she didn't care. 'So what are you doing here? You made your feelings very clear yesterday. Why don't you just leave me alone to get on with my life independently, Rocco?'

He was crouching down beside her and his face was

very close—those bright eyes burning into her like twin blue lasers. 'I'm here to tell you something you need to hear, which is that I love you, Nicole. Very, very much.'

His words were like a red rag to a bull. How dared he say such things so carelessly? Furiously, Nicole shook her head, pulling back from him so that she couldn't be influenced by the warmth of his breath or his proximity. 'You don't love me. You don't love anyone except yourself and your wretched business.'

'I love you,' he repeated fiercely. 'And I want to do all those things you suggested in the lemon grove. To start over. To be with you. And to spend the rest of my life making up for everything I've done, or failed to do.'

Nicole shook her head, trying to cling onto some sense of normality, despite the fact that one of the air stewards was now speaking into the intercom and any minute now he was going to get kicked off the plane— and so, probably, would she. Didn't he realise she didn't have the kind of funds to keep buying more tickets? Did he even *care*? 'It's too late for all that, Rocco. Don't you understand? It's just too late.'

'It can't be,' he said stubbornly.

'It can be whatever I want it to be,' she said, with equal stubbornness.

After a moment he nodded, as if he'd come to some kind of decision, and then he began to talk in a low voice. 'In Monaco you asked whether I had married you because you were pregnant and I said yes.' He voice became more fervent. 'But the main reason I was willing to marry you wasn't just because of duty or the life you carried inside you, but because with you, for the first and only time in my life, I had experienced the *colpe di fulmine*—'

Nicole frowned because for some reason all the passengers within earshot—far from seeming irritated at their delayed take-off—were now cheering wildly.

'What are you talking about?' she snapped.

'The thunderclap,' he interpreted, punching his fist hard against his heart. 'When love strikes like lightning—so intense and powerful that it cannot be denied.'

Nicole blinked at him in sheer amazement. Was this really Rocco—cold, emotionless Rocco Barberi—declaring his feelings and his love for her in front of a *plane-load of people*? 'Why are people cheering?' she questioned suspiciously.

'Because Sicilians are by nature romantic and they enjoy a love story.'

'Well, it's still too late. And now the captain has appeared and is putting on his cap and walking towards us and you really *are* going to get into trouble.'

'Please, *tesoro*.' He cast a wry glance over his shoulder. 'Can we at least go somewhere else and talk about this? I may own the airline but I really don't want the plane to miss its take-off slot.'

He owned the airline?

Nicole blinked.

Was there really no escaping the influence of Rocco Barberi on this infernal island?

She told herself to say no. To tell him she didn't need him—and maybe she didn't. But deep down she wanted him and something told her that was never going to change.

'Very well,' she said grudgingly. 'I will hear you out—just as long as you understand that I'm not making any promises.'

'I understand,' he said gravely.

But despite the clapping which accompanied them as they made their way off the plane, Nicole refused to give the laughing passengers the fairy-tale ending she suspected they wanted. A prolonged kiss in slo-mo and the big clinch on the Tarmac. Because life wasn't a fairy tale and she still didn't believe she had any kind of future with Rocco.

He ushered her towards an unmarked door and before she knew it they were in some sort of private lounge, with huge potted palms, squishy sofas and panoramic views over the runway. But instead of feeling overwhelmed or joyous—or any of the emotions she might have felt if he'd said these things just eighteen hours earlier—Nicole felt flat. More than that, she was angry with herself for allowing herself to be led off a flight which *she* had paid for—like some docile little mouse. Wasn't she supposed to have shed her mouse-like skin?

'So hurry up and say whatever it is you want to say, Rocco.'

It wasn't the most promising of beginnings. In fact, Rocco would go so far as to say that he had never seen Nicole look so angry. And he knew then that he needed to go further than he'd planned. Further than he'd ever been before. That she would not be willing to accept half-measures—and why should she? He'd pushed her away so many times—why would she believe he had changed unless he was prepared to show her? Unless he opened up a heart which had remained locked and bolted for so many years.

He sucked in a deep breath. 'You accused me of pushing you away once we were married and maybe I did—but not for the reasons you imagined. It wasn't because I didn't want you, Nicole—there hasn't been a second of my life since we first met that I didn't want you—but because I was being cautious.'

'Cautious?' She fixed him with an enquiring look.

Restlessly, he shrugged. 'I had no idea how to deal with a pregnant woman—and you were sick. So very sick. I thought you would prefer a nurse rather than a husband who was out of his depth, and then...' He swallowed. 'Then you lost the baby...'

'And *that* was when you pushed me away—'

'I was giving you space,' he argued. 'I thought that's what you needed. I could see how broken you were and I couldn't get near you.'

'You didn't want to get near me,' she said slowly.

'It wasn't that. You wouldn't talk. You wouldn't even look at me. I thought if I went to the States to work that you would have the chance to come to terms with it in your own time.' He sighed. 'And maybe deep down I was relieved that you didn't want to talk about it.'

She tilted her chin to meet his gaze full on. 'Why?'

There was a pause. 'Because I was afraid,' he admitted. 'Afraid of facing my feelings about losing our baby. Afraid of where it might take me.'

The husky choke of his voice made Nicole's heart twist and she wanted to wrap her arms around him and hold him tight. But not yet. Because he needed to do this. To say it and feel it, no matter how much it hurt.

'I was afraid that it would bring up all that stuff from the past when my parents were killed. Stuff I had suppressed and didn't want to look at. Naively, I thought that if I went away—everything would have calmed down by the time I got back.'

'You went to America,' she said woodenly.

He nodded. 'Yes, I did. Which only made it worse. And then I came back to Sicily and—'

'I had gone,' she finished.

'Se.' His features looked like a tight mask. 'I tried telling myself it was all for the best. That I'd never planned for this marriage to happen. I knew I could never make you the kind of husband you wanted. The kind of husband you richly deserved.'

'And that's why you never came after me?'

He nodded. 'That's why I never came after you. Until that divorce petition landed on my desk and suddenly my lifelong ability to suppress my emotions was blown out of the water. I felt anger—and indignation, too. I convinced myself that I was going to get you to come to Monaco with me, because that would be the last thing you wanted. I intended to punish you by making you jump through hoops to get your divorce. I even convinced myself that my desire for you was no more— mainly because my ego had been wounded by having a woman leave me, the way you did.'

He paused. 'And then I saw you... I saw you and the thunderclap happened all over again and there didn't seem to be a thing I could do about it, no matter how much I fought it. I told myself that having sex with you would rid me of my hunger, but it only increased it. Just as being with you reminded me of all the things I love about you. Your creativity. Your irreverence. The way you make me laugh. All those things reinforced what I was reluctant to admit—even to myself.' There was a pause. 'That I love you and want to be with you. Now and always.'

She didn't say anything but her gaze was very steady as she looked at him.

'Could we start again, Nicole?' he said huskily. 'Or continue where we left off? Is spending the rest of your life with me something you would ever consider?'

Her lips seemed to be closing in on themselves and as he saw her struggling to contain her emotions, Rocco desperately ached to hold her, but he knew he must not. Because the answer to his question had to come of its own accord. Not because he was stroking her or kissing her. It needed to come from the mind and the heart, not the body.

Say yes, he prayed silently. *Say yes, my love.*

It seemed to take an eternity but eventually she nodded. 'Yes, I would,' she said, in a rush. 'Of course I would. For all my life if you want it. Oh, Rocco... Rocco,' she said falteringly.

'Let it out, *tesoro*,' he prompted shakily, though he knew he had no right to tell her to connect with *her* emotions when he'd been so cut off from his own for so long. But Nicole's emotions had been repressed too— and wasn't she as much of a novice in all this stuff as he was? 'Just let it out.'

His soft entreaty must have worked because that was when she started to cry—great big tears welling up from those beautiful green eyes and sliding down her cheeks like rain. He held out his arms and she went into them, burying her head against his shoulder while he smoothed down the wild tumble of her curls. She cried until there were no tears left and he suspected she was crying for their lost baby as well as for the wasted years apart. And when he had dried her cheeks with his fingertips, he touched his lips very gently to hers.

'Where we live and how we live is up to you. Tell me what you want and where you want to go,' he said unevenly. 'And I will do everything in my power to make that happen.'

Her eyes were very bright and for the first time a smile lifted the corners of her lips. 'I don't care where we go or what we do,' she said simply. 'The places or the trappings aren't important. I only want to be with you, Rocco. That's all I've ever really wanted.'

EPILOGUE

ROCCO'S VOICE WAS thick with emotion. '*Tesoro*, he is…
bello.'

'Isn't he?' Nicole looked down into the crib at the
sleeping baby, then gazed up into the proud eyes of his
doting papa. 'And the image of his father.'

'Then let us hope he has his mother's good heart
and sense,' responded her husband drily as he pulled
her into his arms, smoothing his hand over the crown
of her head. 'I thought today went well, didn't you?'

Brushing her lips against his neck in a drifting kiss,
Nicole smiled. Today had been their son's baptism—a
joyous day, celebrated first in the Sicilian church where
she and Rocco had been married all those years ago, and
then afterwards at a champagne reception outside, in
the fragrant lemon grove on the Barberi complex. They
had named their son Turi in honour of the patriarch who
had died peacefully last year—contented to see Rocco
and Nicole reunited at last and taking great pleasure in
the role he had played to help bring that about.

Turi hadn't lived to see his great-grandson, but he
had doted on the twin girls who had been born exactly

a year after Nicole and Rocco had decided to make their permanent home in Sicily, albeit with trips to Cornwall whenever their schedules allowed. With their raven corkscrew curls and bright blue eyes, little Lucia and Sofia would have melted the heart of any statue, but they had adored Rocco's grandfather, who had been their biggest fan.

'It was a perfect day,' Nicole said softly. '*Perfetto*. I liked your brother's latest girlfriend and I thought your sister looked very well.'

So much had happened since that day when Rocco had walked onto the aircraft and declared his love for her in front of a planeload of passengers. Approaching their future in an orderly way, her husband had accompanied her back to Cornwall, to help her find someone to take over her little shop—someone who would cherish it as much as she had done.

They had returned to resume their married life in Sicily—not just because Turi was old and frail, but because Nicole found herself valuing the simplicity of life there. And this time she felt she belonged. This time she was no longer the outsider with no legitimate place. Rocco had sold the Monaco apartment and started delegating as much work as possible, in order to spend as much time with the people who really mattered.

His family. The twin daughters who had him wrapped around their little fingers, and now his new son. And Nicole, of course. A day didn't pass without him telling her that she was key to his happiness and none of this could have happened without her.

He had built her a studio with a kiln where, whenever Lucia and Sofia allowed her a rare spare moment, Nicole would craft the vases and the bowls which were gaining her something of a reputation. She had already exhibited in Palermo and Rocco had spoken about buying her a shop there, but she'd told him not to rush anything. That there was a time and a place for ambition and she wanted to enjoy the gifts she had been given. She wanted to give silent thanks that three children had now worn a little romper suit which had lain unused in a drawer for so long…

'Are you sleepy, *tesoro*?' Rocco's softly accented voice broke into her thoughts.

She shook her head. 'Not in the slightest.'

'Then shall we sit outside? Drink some *limonata* on the terrace and watch the stars unfold?'

The complex was quiet after the excitement of the party, which had included most of the villagers and gone on throughout the afternoon and well into the evening. Nicole had listened to smatterings of conversation and had understood most of them, because she had quickly realised that becoming fluent in her husband's language was a necessity and not a hobby. She recognised that communication was key, so she had knuckled down to regular one-to-one lessons with a local schoolteacher and was growing more confident with each day. It amused Rocco no end to hear his English wife calling to him in dialect!

The ice was chinking in her glass and the sweet-sharp *limonata* made from the estate's lemons was cool and refreshing. Above them the darkening indigo sky had begun to glimmer with the promise of the brightest stars Nicole had ever seen and she sighed.

Did Rocco hear her? Was that why his head turned towards her.

'Felici?' he questioned softly.

'Oh, yes. Totally happy,' she said.

Rocco smiled. Who would have realised he could find everything he wanted here, in the arms of his beautiful wife, amid his rapidly expanding family? Sometimes he thought about how much Nicole had taught him. How to face up to your feelings, even if they brought you pain—because with pain came understanding and, from that, true contentment. She had taught him how to love and in so doing had taught him how to live.

He glanced over at her, where she had kicked off her sandals and was wiggling toes which were painted a violent shade of orange. She tied her hair back much more frequently these days because the twins tended to use the thick strands like ropes—but tonight she had shaken the curls free so that they flowed down her back in a dark cascade. Her ankle-length dress in filmy pink chiffon was still more Boho than classic, but that was okay. She looked beautiful in whatever she wore—and she was an artist, after all.

She glanced up to find his gaze trained on her and raised her eyebrows.

'What?' she said.

He moved his shoulders a little restlessly as the heat in his body began to rise. 'I was just wondering if perhaps we might have an early night…'

The answering glint in her eyes answered his question and as he rose from his chair she held up her hands so that he could pull her to her feet.

'You must have read my mind,' she whispered.

'I wonder if you can read mine?' came his answering growl.

She giggled. 'Rocco Barberi, you are a terrible man.'

'I know,' he said, lacing his fingers in hers and leading her towards their house. 'And that's one of the reasons why you love me.'

* * * * *

MILLS & BOON

Coming next month

IMPRISONED BY THE
GREEK'S RING
Caitlin Crews

Atlas was a primitive man, when all was said and done. And whatever else happened in this dirty game, Lexi was his.

Entirely his, to do with as he wished.

He kissed her and he kissed her. He indulged himself. He toyed with her. He tasted her. He was unapologetic and thorough at once.

And with every taste, every indulgence, Atlas felt.

He felt.

He, who hadn't felt a damned thing in years. He, who had walled himself off to survive. He had become stone. Fury in human form.

But Lexi tasted like hope.

"This doesn't feel like revenge," she whispered in his ear, and she sounded drugged.

"I'm delighted you think so," he replied.

And then he set his mouth to hers again, because it was easier. Or better. Or simply because he had to, or die wanting her.

Lexi thrashed beneath him, and he wasn't sure why until he tilted back his head to get a better look at her face. And the answer slammed through him like some kind of cannonball, shot straight into him.

Need. She was wild with need.

And he couldn't seem to get enough of it. Of her.

The part of him that trusted no one, and her least of all, didn't trust this reaction either.

But the rest of him—especially the hardest part of him—didn't care.

Because she tasted like magic and he had given up on magic long, long time ago.

Because her hands tangled in his hair and tugged his face to hers, and he didn't have it in him to question that.

All Atlas knew was that he wanted more. Needed more.

As if, after surviving things that no man should be forced to bear, it would be little Lexi Haring who took him out. It would be this one shockingly pretty woman who would be the end of him. And not because she'd plotted against him, as he believed some if not all of her family had done, but because of this. Her surrender.

The endless, wondrous glory of her surrender.

Continue reading
IMPRISONED BY THE
GREEK'S RING
Caitlin Crews

LET'S TALK
Romance

For exclusive extracts, competitions
and special offers, find us online:

f facebook.com/millsandboon

⊙ @millsandboonuk

🐦 @millsandboon

Or get in touch on 0844 844 1351*

For all the latest titles coming soon, visit
millsandboon.co.uk/nextmonth